Haley's Hero

Lake Ozark Ladies, Book 3

By Helen Gray

HALEY'S HERO

ISBN-10:1-944203-23-0

ISBN-13:978-1-944203-23-8

And they took offense at him. But Jesus said to them, A prophet is not without honor except in his own town and in his own home. Matthew 13:57 (NIV)

Chapter 1

"*G*ood morning, Pistol."

The black Labrador sat on his haunches, waiting at his daily spot, as Haley West hoofed it to the corner of Iris and Fourth. Rain or shine, the dog accompanied the mail carrier around the west side of town in his self-appointed escort service.

Haley smiled and hitched the mail bag higher on her shoulder. "Come on, boy, let's go."

He followed her and waited while she went up the steps of the next house, stuffed two letters and a sale flyer in the mailbox attached next to the door, and returned to the sidewalk.

Hot and dry, the late June Tuesday burned with unaccustomed heat that encased Haley like a hot cocoon. She inhaled the scent of heat-softened asphalt and glanced up at the sun, readjusting the baseball style cap of her postal uniform. Her dark blue shorts were knee length, and a coordinating light blue shirt bore a U. S. Postal insignia like the one on the cap.

Making good time on the short blocks, Haley hiked up the street of her hometown with Pistol trotting alongside her. Skyview, Missouri, was located in the countryside within a stone's throw of the Lake of the Ozarks, as her mother used to say. Haley reached into the mailbag for another bundle of envelopes. Walking slowly and looking down as she removed the rubber band from around them, she jerked her head up when Pistol growled. He grabbed her sock with his teeth and tugged.

At that moment a bicycle topped the hill and came careening down the street. As it passed Haley, a handlebar clipped the strap of her mailbag and jerked it off her shoulder. She managed to wrest it clear and hang onto it, but staggered to stay upright as the bicycle whizzed on down the hill. The kid riding it appeared to be no more than seven or eight, and the bike was a bit too big for him. He pedaled furiously, his stout body moving side to side as his short legs worked their way round and round. The bike wove from one side of the road to the other, wobbling out of control as it passed the intersection of Third Street.

Haley had barely registered those brief facts when the runaway bike hit the railroad tracks that crossed the street, and went airborne.

Pistol yipped and set off at a run as the boy and bike toppled beside the road. Haley hefted the bag strap back up onto her shoulder while running after the dog. She landed on her knees beside the boy and placed a hand on his shoulder.

He lay still. Haley wasn't sure if he was hurt or just winded, but his left leg rested at an awkward angle above his body, the toe of his tennis shoe caught in the spokes of the rear wheel.

The boy opened his eyes and stared up at her in what struck Haley as sheer terror. She recognized the round face, small chin, and almond shaped eyes of Dennis Bailey. "Stay still," she cautioned in a calming tone. "Let's see if you're hurt."

She ran a hand over his leg, and drew back when he flinched. "Does that hurt?"

He didn't say a word, just stared up at her as if she were a monster about to end his days. "Is your leg hurt?" she repeated, pulling her cell phone from her pocket.

The sound of a vehicle coming toward the tracks drew her attention. The hearse?

Good grief, the boy wasn't dead.

As the thought flashed through her mind, the long black vehicle stopped near the tracks, and a man emerged from it. If Haley had been chewing gum, she would have swallowed it. Neil Bronson was back in town?

She would have known him instantly, even if he hadn't been driving the hearse from the Bronson Mortuary, the business his parents had operated for many years. But he lived in St. Louis. What was he doing back in Skyview?

Haley forced air into her lungs as he trotted across the street. "What are you doing here?"

"I started to turn at the funeral home when I looked up the street and saw the bike hit the tracks." He squatted next to her and eyed the boy, assessing him.

Pistol circled them, whining. Then he stopped and licked one of the kid's hands.

The boy looked up at the dog, his chin quivering. Then a hand crept up to the furry animal's black nose that had a white spot about the size of a dime on it, the only part of the dog that wasn't black. "Pistol," he whimpered, raising his head.

"Keep still," Neil ordered gently, a hand on a shoulder keeping the boy prone. Then he returned his attention to Haley. "I didn't know you were back here, Haley."

She ignored the comment and nodded at the boy. "This is Dennis Bailey."

His brow creased. "The police chief's grandson?"

She indicated her phone. "I had just started to call him." She found the number of the police department and called it, doing her best to concentrate.

Neil gripped the boy's shoe and tugged at it gently. When it didn't come out of the spokes, he untied it and carefully worked the foot free.

Dennis stopped crying and darted a look up the hill behind them, as if searching for something—or someone.

"Deputy Collins. May I help you?"

Haley forced her attention onto the phone. "Hi, Brad. This is Haley West. There's been a little accident over here at the railroad tracks just behind the funeral home. A boy had a bicycle wreck, and his foot may be hurt."

"By chance is it Dennis?" The deputy's tone was wry.

"Yes. Is his grandpa there?"

"He's out looking for Dennis. The boy's babysitter called and said he disappeared. I'll call and let the chief know where to find you."

"Thanks." Haley disconnected and returned her attention to Dennis, who was being thoroughly examined by Neil.

"I think he's okay," Neil pronounced, cradling the boy in an arm. "The ankle may be sore for a few days."

"His grandpa should be here soon."

"No-o-o-o." Dennis wailed and sat up, his lips quivering.

"Hey, buddy, Grandpa loves you, and he'll take care of you."

"Dennis ...in trouble ...'gin." He rubbed his eyes with the back of a hand.

Neil gave him a hug. "I bet your grandpa won't be mad. I know him."

Dennis looked up at Neil, his attention caught. "You do?"

Neil nodded. "I do. He's a nice guy, and he'll be happy to see that you're okay."

Dennis looked over at the bike, and his face crumpled again. "The bike's hurt. Tommy will be mad."

Neil looked over the boy's head at Haley and mouthed, "Brother?"

She nodded. "Tommy is a couple years older than Dennis. They live over in the Greenwood Apartments." She returned her attention to Dennis. "Is it Tommy's bike?"

Dennis dipped his head. "Uh, huh."

"I don't think the bike's hurt. Okay?"

His eyes brightened with hope. "Okay."

A police car sped up the street and stopped at the tracks. Chief Richards, a six foot four gentle giant, emerged and joined them. He stooped and took Dennis from Neil. "Hey, big guy, what have you been doing?"

A guarded expression came over the boy's face. His eyes darted back up the hill again, his expression fearful. Had he been running from someone? The very idea made Haley angry. A handicapped child like Dennis was easy to bully.

Down's Syndrome children, while unconditionally loving, were childlike and dependent. They needed protection. And she would help protect Dennis if she found out that other children were mistreating him.

"Thanks for looking after my boy," the chief said, standing erect with Dennis in his arms. "I'll take him by the clinic and have Doc Gaines look him over."

"Would you like me to put that in the trunk of your car?" Neil indicated the bike.

"I'd appreciate it."

He went to get the bike, and Pistol followed him.

"I need to get moving," Haley called over her

shoulder, heading back up the street.

She had reached Fourth Street when footsteps pounded behind her. A hand touched her arm. "Wait up."

Haley stopped and turned to face Neil Bronson, Pistol at his feet. Her breath caught in her throat. Always a good-looking guy, he appeared more filled out than the teenage boy of her memory. Long trim legs and well-developed shoulders and torso bore evidence of rigorous physical training. He had the look of a man now, dressed in dark loafers, dark slacks, and a white shirt with the sleeves rolled halfway up his forearms.

"Don't act like we've never met, Haley West," he chided in a lightly teasing tone.

His deep voice made her mouth go dry. She inhaled a long fortifying breath and met his gaze. "What are you doing back here, Neil?"

Even white teeth flashed. "My mother's having more surgery, and Dad's not well. I took a few weeks of family leave to be with them and see if I can be of any help."

Haley breathed easier. He was only here temporarily. By sheer force of will she kept her stiff smile in place. "I heard that your mother isn't doing well, but I didn't know her condition had become so serious. I'm sorry."

"Children have a God-given responsibility to look after their parents. Eric can't do everything. I have to help, and make some decisions."

"Don't you have a job elsewhere?" Her tongue

nearly stuck to the roof of her dry mouth. She knew very well he did, having subscribed to the local newspaper and read about him over the years.

He nodded. "I'm director of a YMCA in St. Louis. It's nice to see you again."

"Nice to see you, too." *Not really. Well, maybe.*

"I saw the way you came flying down the hill after that kid. I also saw him almost jerk your arm off and knock you down. How is your shoulder?"

Haley winced slightly and gave it a rub. "It may be a little sore tomorrow, but nothing to worry about. If it is, I'll just carry the bag on my other shoulder."

He scrutinized her in detail. "You look good. I had no idea you walked the streets here." He grinned at his little pun.

"Did you think Dennis acted like he was scared?" she asked, needing to direct the subject away from herself.

His expression sobered. "As a matter of fact, I did. Any idea why?"

"I wondered if other kids might have been giving him a hard time, but most of the ones I know around here seem to accept him and like him. I'm sure you remember his mother, Cindy."

He nodded. "I remember her well."

"She's a single mother and works in the clinic pharmacy. The chief will go straight to her before seeing the doctor." Haley mustered a smile and gave a meaningful glance at her watch. "I'm running late. I'd better get moving."

She hitched the bag higher on her shoulder and

took off. This time he didn't follow. Except in her thoughts. Neil Bronson. High school heartthrob. Two years older than her, which would make him thirty-one now. And the one person she was certain knew about her humiliation over Rick. But he didn't know how much it had damaged her already fragile self-esteem.

Haley had developed a crush on Neil after the experience with Rick, but had gotten over it when she learned that he also was a rat. She had learned her lesson well. Men were not to be trusted. She would make no more such mistakes—never risk that kind of pain again.

As she and Pistol continued the route, an avalanche of unwanted memories assaulted Haley. High school. Being shunned or ignored by the popular kids—subtle in nature, but nevertheless kept outside the inner circles. The exceptions had been Paige and Kelsey, whose friendship from church had carried over into their school world.

Neil, on the other hand, had been the star at anything he did. Good looking, athletic, and moneyed, he was part of those who took privilege for granted, had his choice of dates and friends. Yet he had never seemed arrogant like many of the popular set. He and his brother Eric, who was now principal of the local high school, had attended church with their parents and been good students and athletes, so they could march to their own drummer and get no flack.

Having Neil around, even for a few weeks, could be a distraction and keep her on edge. Haley didn't need that. She had to keep her priorities straight, concentrate on why she had returned here.

Back at the post office that afternoon, Haley finished up her work, checked out, and went home. She had her head on straight now. She had a disabled mother in the nursing home whose legal affairs and details of her care were Haley's responsibility, a family that needed her, and a job that made it possible for her to be independent. She would be content.

Her dream of having someone to love her, a home and family of her own, had grown dimmer and dimmer. Hard work, prayer, and time with her friends and family must fill the emptiness inside her.

~

Neil drove around the block and parked the hearse behind the mortuary, his mood pensive. Running into Haley had been a blast from the past. He couldn't get over how pretty she had grown, her girlhood insecurities and imperfections polished away by time and maturity.

He remembered her as quiet and studious, the kind of girl who always handed in her assignments on time, or early—a regular on the honor roll. A bit of a shy wallflower, she had been an easy target for Rick's flattery. She might have changed physically with age, but he had detected the same gentle spirit.

He climbed into his truck and drove to his parents' house.

"I've got supper ready," his dad called from the kitchen. "If you'll pour the tea and set the table while I set the food on it, we can eat."

"How long has Haley West been back in town?"

Neil asked after they were seated and his dad had asked the blessing.

Jim Bronson pursed his mouth and paused in adding sweetener to his tea. "Let's see. It was right after that bad wreck that killed her sister and put her mother in the nursing home. Guess it must have been about two years ago."

Neil frowned. "I knew about her sister's death, but I didn't know how badly her mother was injured."

His dad grimaced. "Her back was broken and her head banged up. She's in a wheelchair, paralyzed from the waist down, and brain damaged. The younger sister was still in high school. She's in college now, I'm guessing with Haley's support."

"Haley always had a difficult life. I kind of admired her, but felt sorry for her, all at the same time."

"Don't ever let her hear you say that. The part about feeling sorry for her, I mean."

Neil nodded. "Gotcha. She's a chin-up kind of gal, and I'm sure pity would bug her."

"Make her mad as a hatter. She's a tough cookie."

"And smart." She had been bright—and cute.

Dad nodded. "Even I remember that she was salutatorian of her class. Too bad she's had such a load to carry. I take it you saw her today." He phrased it as a question.

Neil related the incident that had caused their meeting.

"Sam Richards has his hands full helping his daughter with that boy. With both boys," he amended with a shake of his head. "Since Cindy's husband left her, she has to work full-time instead of part-time. Sam does what he can for them, but the older boy has a strong will, and Cindy has a hard time keeping him in line. I see him running around town with a group of boys who have a talent for mischief. The younger one is sweet, but he needs extra attention."

After supper Neil helped his dad clean up—while his mind clamored with questions. Why had he reacted like a teenager at seeing Haley again? How should he help his parents? He and Eric didn't want to abandon Mom and Dad, but neither of them had any desire to carry on a family business centered on death. What had frightened that little boy?

Haley moved back here to take care of her family.

That's why I'm here, but my circumstances are different.

His eyes automatically rose to stare at his and Beth's wedding picture that graced the wall facing them. It had been four years since her death, and they had been hard. Beyond hard. Devastating. Every time he thought he had his life back together, he took another nosedive. Overwhelmed by memories and grief, he had left and planned to never return to Skyview. But his parents needed him now. His mother's rheumatoid arthritis had spread through her body, and his dad's health wasn't good enough for him to keep taking care of her the way he had for years. Neil experienced a sudden sense of kinship with Haley West. If anyone would understand, she was the one.

~

Haley arrived home that evening, exhausted and

mentally drained. Home was a little three-bedroom house in a subdivision at the east edge of town. Although small, it provided all the space she needed. One bedroom had been converted into a den with a sofa and television. She also had her desk and computer in there.

After a quick meal of leftovers and an ice cream bar, she checked her e-mail and watched the news. Then she showered and crawled into bed.

Wednesday Haley delivered the mail as usual. When she returned to the post office, Vince, the postmaster, greeted her with a grin and pointed at the folded newspaper on the counter. "You made the news in a roundabout way."

Published weekly, the *Skyview Banner* went in the mailboxes on Thursday mornings, but it was delivered to the post office, local stores, and mechanical dispensers Wednesday afternoon. Haley put away her empty mail trays and stored her scanner before picking up the new edition.

Mrs. Ruth Mohler had complained at the City Council meeting Tuesday night about the number of children riding their bikes up and down the streets and causing accidents, such as the one she had observed when a biker had nearly hit their lady mail carrier and had a wreck on the railroad tracks. The woman also reported that people in that part of town were having a problem with petty vandalisms around their properties.

When she finished the article, Haley chuckled and tossed the paper back onto the counter. "The kids have to occupy themselves during the summer. I'd rather see them out getting physical exercise than spending all their time watching TV and playing video games."

Vince nodded. "I agree."

She eyed the paper. "I wonder if it bothered Darlene Fowler to have to write that article." Darlene was the Banner's only reporter.

Vince's brows arched. "Why would it bother her?"

Haley heaved a sigh. Vince had only been their postmaster about ten years and didn't know the history of everyone in town. "Back in high school she got pregnant by a boy who died in a motorcycle accident. She married someone else before the baby was born, but it didn't last. There's been another marriage, baby, and divorce since then. She's a single mother of two boys, and they're on the streets a lot."

His mouth widened in understanding. "On their bikes?"

She nodded. Mention of Darlene resurrected memories of Haley's personal humiliation and hurt. She didn't know for sure if Darlene knew about Rick's dalliance with her, but Darlene's coolness toward her over the years made Haley suspect she did. Haley had died an inner death at that funeral—and never looked back.

Thursday morning Haley overslept and arrived at work without a minute to spare. The truck driver from the distribution center had just pulled into the parking lot. Within minutes he had the truck unloaded and had gone on to his next stop. She sorted several feet of mail into separate bins for each route. Then it had to be cased into batches and put in order by addresses. She was done when Vince and the other carrier arrived. It took three trips to load the mail truck.

Haley drove across the railroad tracks and parked on Fourth. Then she hiked a loop of two blocks and returned to the truck. She unlocked the door, tossed the mailbag inside, and started to get behind the wheel when the sound of loud, argumentative voices made her hesitate and look around. As she did, something whizzed through the air.

Pain exploded inside her head.

Chapter 2

*H*aley clutched at the steering wheel, and then the edge of the seat, as she slid downward, fighting to stay on her feet. The truck keys slipped from her fingers. Dimly she heard a vehicle approaching.

My head is broken.

She slumped to the ground, holding a hand across the side of her head while patting the ground with the other hand. As she touched the key ring, a van screeched to a halt next to the open door of the truck. Someone hopped out. "Are you okay, honey?"

Haley peered up at Mrs. Mohler, who lived two blocks over. The portly, gray haired woman bent at the waist and peered down at her through eyes big as saucers behind round, orange tinted glasses. "You're hurt. How can I help?"

Haley tried to say it wasn't necessary, but groaned and sat motionless, waiting for her vision to clear and her head to stop spinning. "Call Vince," she finally managed to choke.

"I'll call the police, too." The woman scurried away.

Moments later she returned. "I called Vince and told him you're hurt. Then I called the police. Just stay still, sweetie." Her voice was small and high pitched for such a large woman.

Haley started to nod, but stopped when it made her head pound.

"Don't move, sweetie. They're on their way. Is there anything else I can do? Can I help you get up?"

Haley reached for the woman's outstretched hand and started to get to her feet, but a wave of dizziness made her sink back to the ground. She held out the key. "Will you lock the truck for me?" She had to make sure the mail was secure, in case she passed out.

A siren screamed in the distance.

"Of course, dear." She locked the door and was returning the key when a police car came flying up the street and stopped near the truck. Without moving, Haley stared over at its wheels.

"I called her boss like she asked," Ruth Mohler told the officer who came running toward them. "Should I call an ambulance?"

"Let me check on her." He got down on his hands and knees, and Haley met the intense blue eyes of white haired Chief Richards. Behind him stood Neil Bronson. The chief's face screwed up in a frown when he removed her hand from her head and inspected it. "You've got quite a knot. What happened?"

"Something hit me, I think a rock. I don't know where it came from."

"Let's put you in my car and take you to the clinic."

"That isn't necessary," Haley protested. "I'll be fine. And I can't leave before Vince gets here."

"Here he comes."

Neil's voice made her gaze up at him. In spite of her fuddled condition, the sight of his powerfully built frame made her feel as if she had been punched in the gut. Why, oh why, did he always have to be around when she was at her absolute worst?

"Hey, what are you doing sitting down on the job?" Vince joked as he appeared behind the two men. He frowned when he saw the knot on her head. "I'll get the mail. You get medical attention. That's an order."

When she opened her mouth to protest, her boss raised a palm. "No, you're going to the clinic, and you're not coming back to work. Not today. I'll have Debby finish your route. You can call me after you've seen a doctor and we'll discuss tomorrow."

Haley had no fight left in her. She let the chief and Neil each clasp one of her arms and ease her to her feet. They assisted her into the back seat of the police car, and Neil slid in beside her.

Within minutes they escorted her into the medical clinic, and a nurse took her directly to an examination room. Doctor Gaines checked the bump on her head and pronounced her able to go home, *if* she followed orders to take it easy the rest of the day and take the pain medication he prescribed.

The doctor handed her a prescription slip. "You're going to have a doozy of a headache if you don't take those pills, but you don't have a concussion."

~

When a nurse beckoned them from a doorway, Neil accompanied Sam Richards into the room where Haley sat on the side of an examination table. He had been at the police station, talking to his dad's old friend about the damage someone had done to the hearse, when the call had come in about Haley. When Sam told him where he was going, Neil had asked to tag along. He carried her postal cap in his right hand.

Haley frowned when she saw them, her blue eyes stormy. She had a nasty bruise near her right temple and looked fragile, yet still lovely. Neil wanted to know who had done this to her, to chase the shadows from her eyes. She kept so much bottled up inside her.

"May we take her home?" Richards asked the doctor.

He nodded. "See that she takes it easy. After a good night's sleep she should be fine."

Neil held out the hat. "I picked this up off the ground. Thought you might like to have it back."

"And here's your purse." Chief Richards placed it on the table beside her. "Vince took it from the truck and asked me to give it to you."

Haley gave the chief a nod and reached for the hat, as if Neil might bite her. Her face reminded Neil of his last conversation with her in high school. She had been battered then as well, only not in a physical sense.

A classmate of his had admitted to seeing Haley on the sly, leading her on while Darlene considered him her steady. He and Rick had argued about it, and Neil had threatened to personally punch Rick's lights out if he hurt Haley.

But he hadn't gotten a chance.

"Thanks." She didn't meet his eyes as she took the hat. He thought he understood. Meeting again after all this time had to resurrect painful memories for her.

He had always thought her attractive. Now her almost black hair had the stylish cut it had lacked back then. She shoved the cap over it.

He started to assist her from the table, but she slid to the floor before he could do so. He watched her nearly lose her balance and place a hand on the table for a moment to steady herself. They walked out of the clinic together, and he assisted her back into the police car.

"I assume you have a vehicle on the post office parking lot," he said once he had buckled her seat belt, rounded the car, and slid onto the seat beside her.

She nodded and eased back into the seat, her purse clutched to her chest.

"I'll drive her home," he informed the chief.

In front of them, the chief nodded. "That sounds like a good idea." He started the motor. At the post office he pulled around to the back edge of the lot where Haley's white Chevy Tracker was parked.

Neil placed a hand on her arm and escorted her from the police car to the Tracker. "I need your keys," he said when she was in the passenger seat.

She handed them to him without argument and rode in silence for a couple of blocks. She looked over at him when he turned into her subdivision without asking for directions.

"I asked Sam where you live," he explained simply. "Are you renting or buying?"

"Buying." She shoved her purse under one arm, as if ready to bolt. Then she frowned. "How will you get back to your car? Do you need to borrow mine?"

He flashed a grin at her and made a wide swing into the driveway of her corner lot house. "I called Eric, and he's picking me up."

As if by magic, a blue pickup appeared in the street behind them.

"We're going to visit Mom in the hospital. Then I'll retrieve my car from the police station." He pulled the keys from the ignition and held them out to her. "Let me help you inside and get you an ice pack."

She drew herself up and took the keys. "I'm fine. I don't need help."

My help. He watched the pain play across her face and heard the effort it took for her to keep her voice steady. But he also recognized sheer determination.

"Go straight to bed and sleep off that headache," he ordered, easing from the vehicle.

Haley turned and headed for the door.

Neil hated to leave her, but she needed to rest, and no way would she allow him inside her house.

~

Thursday morning Haley woke feeling much better. She did the best she could to cover the purple bruise near her temple with makeup before getting dressed. Then she called Vince and told him she would be reporting for work at her regular time.

Pistol joined her at Fourth and Iris as usual. Haley greeted the dog and kept moving. When they reached the spot where she had been hit the day before, she paused and closed her eyes for a moment, trying to recall details. The thing that came to mind was voices—and the sound of them. It had been children. Satisfied that no adult had been stalking her, Haley opened her eyes and surveyed the area. She estimated the direction she had been facing and followed an invisible line to where she thought the rock could have come from.

Satisfied, she continued her way around the block. When she reached the area where she thought the children had been, she studied the surroundings in detail. The grass in this open lot showed evidence of heavy trampling. A privacy fence ran along one side of the half-acre, and an old wagon bed sat before it.

In her mind's eye, Haley envisioned a group of kids playing back here and climbing around on that wagon bed, the kind of activity normal for children out of school for the summer. The troubling aspect was that there had been squabbling—or outright fighting—in progress. Rock throwing was dangerous. Did they even know that someone had been hit? With no answers forming, she continued on her route.

A couple of blocks further, she turned a corner and spied Dennis Bailey sitting, legs outstretched, on the sidewalk in front of the apartments where he lived. He wore a forlorn expression.

Pistol trotted to the boy and licked his chin. Dennis wrapped his short arms around the dog's neck and buried his face in the fur. "Dennis sad," he mumbled.

Haley wanted to comfort the boy, but decided that Pistol had the matter under control. She kept walking, surmising that Dennis had lost his biking privileges.

Farther up the street, she met the older brother. "Hello, Tommy," she greeted him. "Been having a good time so far this summer?"

The ten-year-old's expression turned wary. "I guess so."

"Is your bike okay?"

He nodded. "It's not smashed. The menace ain't supposed to ride it any more. Can't ride his own for a week either."

"Why was he riding yours instead of his own?"

Tommy shrugged. "I don't know. I guess he was in too big a hurry to look for his own. He forgets where he leaves it."

"Why was he in such a hurry?"

"I dunno." He headed across the street.

Haley kept pace with the boy. "Do you have any idea who was in the lot next to the Stuart house yesterday about that time?"

"No." He walked faster, clearly not wanting to talk to her. Haley slowed and watched him practically run up the block and round the corner out of sight.

After work, Haley didn't go straight home. Instead, she drove to the north part of town and parked at the nursing home. Inside the building, she passed the front offices and crossed the small lobby where two elderly residents, a man and a woman, sat in their wheelchairs staring at a blaring television in the corner of the room.

With a brief smile and a wave to the nurse at the nurses' station next to the doorway, Haley headed down a familiar hallway where the mild scent of antiseptic pervaded. A woman inched alongside the wall in a wheelchair, while an elderly man shuffled along with the aid of a walker. Coming here almost daily and observing these people—many of whom she knew and had grown up with their children or grandchildren—in various stages of decline, was sobering.

At the door of her mother's room, Haley pasted a smile on her face and entered. Violet West lay in bed, her eyes closed. When Haley stood by the bed and placed a hand on her arm, those brown eyes opened, and Mom smiled in recognition.

Haley's heart constricted. Her mother had worked so hard and received so little in return. Over the years she had worked a factory job and cared for her four children, along with shouldering care for her elderly parents.

Mom had taken Haley and her sisters to church with her every Sunday, but Dillon had refused to go with them and stayed home with their dad. Frank West, who did odd jobs around town, had made a profession of faith as a young man, but he had never grown as a Christian and did not attend church with his wife. So how could Mom convince their son to go? Haley knew how much it had troubled her mother, but she understood why Mom had given up the battle.

At eighteen, just out of high school, Dillon had enlisted and been deployed to Afghanistan. During his years in the military, his drinking, which had begun in high school, grew worse. Only twenty-one when he discharged, he had trouble finding work and moved back home. Their dad's death weeks later sent him into despondency, and the drinking worsened even further.

When Mom had wanted to go visit her sister, Dillon had assured her and the girls that he was sober and offered to drive them. The trip and visit had gone fine, but while there, without their knowledge, Dillon had dipped into his stash of booze hidden in the car trunk. On the way home, he lost control of the car and had a wreck that killed Reba and ended normal life for their mother. Dillon and Leann were injured, but they both recovered with no lasting effects.

"Hi, Mom. How are they treating you here?"

Mom tipped her head on the pillow, straining to peer behind Haley. "Frank's here?" Her speech slurred.

"No, Mom. He's not here. It's just me, Haley." It broke her heart to see her mother so helpless and confused that she didn't even remember that her husband had died. Haley continued to carry on a disjointed conversation, just letting her mother know of her love by her presence.

After the visit, Haley walked back to the lobby and left the building. The temperature had cooled to a more pleasant level. She drove home and curled up on the sofa for a nap.

Sometime later the buzz of the doorbell woke her.

Chapter 3

*N*eil jabbed at the doorbell with one hand, while balancing a pizza box with the other. After visiting his mother and finding her alert enough to talk to him for a few minutes before falling asleep, he had surrendered to his odd compulsion to see Haley again. He started to push the buzzer again, but the door eased open. Haley stared out at him, her face wearing a half alert look that told him she had been asleep.

"Are you hungry?" He passed the pizza box before her face so she would get a whiff. "Got any coffee or tea?"

Her eyes brightened as she inhaled the delicious aroma, and she stepped back to admit him. "How can you wave that at me and ask such a question?"

Good. It sounded as if the nap had revived her. He entered and looked around. Her home reflected her personality. Bright, yet casual. Neat and organized. Cozy. It spoke of a sedate, methodical approach to life. Beige carpeting. White walls. A kitchen visible directly ahead, and a hallway to the left. An entertainment center occupied one wall, a navy sofa and glider the other. Open gold drapes revealed a full view of the back yard through a sliding glass door.

His attention returned to Haley's face. "You must have really been tired to go to sleep in your uniform. If you want to change, I'll find my way around your kitchen."

She hesitated a moment, and then yielded. "I'll be right back."

The look of surprise on her face at his arrival with food made him think she didn't get looked after much. Along with that thought came the realization that he wanted to look after her.

Even back in high school he had felt a protective instinct toward her. She had come from a poor family, so he figured her quietness probably stemmed from self-consciousness about her lack of fashionable clothes and spending money. She still seemed quiet, but there was more confidence and self-assurance in her manner.

He found a pitcher of tea in the fridge, paper plates and cups in the cabinets, and had everything arranged on the coffee table when Haley returned to the living room. Appearing more alert, she made a pretty picture in pink slacks and a white tee shirt. She sat on the sofa, her cute dimples doing a number on his concentration.

He scooped a slice of pizza from the box and handed it to her. Then he took one for himself and eased back in the glider facing her. Rather than say anything, he simply bowed his head and said a brief, silent blessing. Then he raised his head and saw her do the same. "Do you like carrying the mail?"

"It's honest work," she said quietly. "I make more than I could at most jobs around here. It's outdoors. Yeah, I like it."

"How long have you been doing it?"

"Two years back here in Skyview. I enlisted after high school and spent eight years in the military. After my discharge, I took the postal exam, getting extra points for being a veteran."

Yeah, like she needed them. She probably scored high enough to make those points totally unnecessary.

"I took the first job offered and went to work for the Springfield post office. I had only been there a few weeks when my family's accident happened, and I took a leave to be with them. Jay Kent let me know that he was about ready to retire from the post office here, so I went ahead and requested a transfer. It came through a few weeks later."

How could so much time have passed? "How are things with your family?"

She shrugged. "Leann finished high school last month and moved to Springfield to start summer classes. There's nothing I can do for Dillon. I visit Mom regularly at the nursing home."

"I had already moved away before it happened, but I heard about the wreck that took your other sister's life. I'm sorry. It had to have been heartbreaking."

The sheen of tears that glistened in her eyes tore at him. He had some idea of the pain and loss she was feeling.

She bit at her lips to stop their trembling. "Reba was more than just my sister. She was my best friend," she said in a tight voice. "We shared a room. Our clothes. Our thoughts and feelings. She was only twenty-one. I miss her."

She swiped at her eyes and stiffened her shoulders. "Since you know about the wreck, you must know that Dillon is in prison. He was driving and lost control of the car. His alcohol level was way over the legal limit. He got six years for gross vehicular manslaughter, but he could get parole any time."

He studied her. "Does that bother you? Do you think he should have to serve the whole sentence?"

She took a deep breath and shook her head. "I'm not his judge. It's between him and God. Leann says he's sober now and means to stay that way."

"You don't make contact with him?"

Her eyes took on a glazed look, the pizza in her hand forgotten. "I can't talk to him. I don't know what to say."

"You need to see him, let him know he's forgiven."

"I know. Mom will never recover, and Reba's gone from our lives until we meet her in heaven. I know we have to go on with our lives. But you know how hard that is. I'm sorry about Beth."

He clamped down on the grief that hearing his wife's name brought. "Life isn't always easy. We do what's necessary. It doesn't seem fair that you've endured so much."

"Nor you. Your mother's condition has to be difficult for you."

"I have to lean on God for strength. I couldn't help but think earlier how much we have in common. The losses of my wife and your sister. Both our mothers in bad health."

Haley shook her head, the glaze in her eyes clearing. She began to eat.

I appreciate this," she said after washing down a bite of pizza with a healthy swig of tea. She wiped her mouth with her napkin.

He did the same. "Have you figured out where the rock came from that hit you?"

She shook her head, frowning. "I saw both the Bailey boys today, though. Dennis was dejected over losing his bike riding privileges for the week. At least I hope that's all it was."

"Me, too."

"I ran into Tommy just up the street from the apartments where Dennis was sitting. He wasn't overly friendly, and he avoided answering when I asked him if he knew what might have been going on in the neighborhood at that time. I'm going to keep my eyes open, especially on the kids. I'm afraid there could be some kind of feud going on up there."

Neil considered what she had said. "You hear and

see a lot of things as you move around town. Do you recall seeing anyone hanging around the funeral home in a suspicious way?"

She took another slice of pizza and bit into it hungrily, chewing and swallowing before speaking. "Nothing out of the ordinary comes to mind. Why?"

He placed his slice of pizza back in the box. "I found some minor damage on the back door of the hearse. Dad says he hasn't had any accidents and doesn't know of any reason it should be scratched. That's what I was talking to Chief Richards about when he got the call about you. I had dropped the matter of the hearse door, but this morning I found more serious damage."

She paused before biting into the pizza again. "What kind of damage?"

"The glass over the sign in front of the business is broken."

She frowned. "I assume you reported it. Sounds to me like you need to return to police work and help Chief Richards find out what's going on around here. You used to work for him, and he has confidence in you."

How did she know so much about him? "That was before Beth died. You weren't living here then."

She hesitated, as if regretting her revelation. "I subscribed to the local newspaper all the years I lived elsewhere."

"Ah, so you kept up with people and happenings." Including him?

She shrugged. "The town in general. After all, I

grew up here, and my family still lived here." She resumed eating, making light of it.

It pleased him to see her putting away his food offering. An idea struck him. "Dad asked me to take over leadership of Teen College at the church for him later this month. He already has plans laid out, but with Mom in the hospital again, he doesn't think he can handle it. If I agree to stay here longer than originally planned and do it, would you help me?"

"Teen College?"

He nodded. "It's a version of Bible School for the youth. You'd be great at it."

She shook her head. "I don't think so."

"Will you at least think about it?"

"I'll think about it," was all she promised. He didn't press further, not wanting to risk getting a flat refusal.

When the rest of the pizza was gone, Haley gathered their debris and dumped it in the trash can in the kitchen. "Thanks for the food." Her tone sounded dismissive.

He took the hint. At the door he turned. "I enjoyed spending this time with you. Maybe we should do it again sometime." He pulled a McDonald's receipt from a pocket, scribbled his cell phone number on the back of it, and held it out to her. "Call me if you need anything."

When she didn't take it, he tossed it on the table. Then he opened the door and stepped out into the balmy evening air. The deadbolt clicked behind him.

~

Haley sagged against the closed door. She loved

kids, but she wasn't teen leadership material. The very idea reminded her of past failures and shortcomings. The events of the day, and now a request like that, had her frustrated.

"Lord, I can't get involved with teenagers—or Neil. You know how hard I worked to get away from here and be independent. Now I'm right back where I started, with everyone depending on me—and still just that poor West girl."

Haley had power of attorney and handled all her mother's paperwork. Leann needed her financial help. She didn't know how to relate to Dillon any more. And now Neil was here.

One of her reasons for leaving Skyview had been to ensure not running into Neil. She had trained herself to not think about him and buried herself in work, but she had always kept tabs on her family. After being played for a fool by Rick as a teenager, and then being infatuated with Neil, who had subsequently married one of the dearest girls around, Haley had accepted that her role would be as a caretaker of others. Love, a husband and family of her own, were not to be.

Yet, somewhere deep inside her, was a growing sense that God had a task for her, a fresh plan for her life. But she had no idea what it could be.

A prophet is not without honour, save in his own country, and in his own house.

Unbidden, the bit of scripture floated into her silent self-examination.

"I'm not a prophet, Lord. I'm just a poor girl who has never quite fit in or been accepted in her hometown."

You're my child. You fit in my kingdom.

Haley closed her eyes. When she did, the image of Neil Bronson's face returned, his penetrating dark eyes and sunshine smile tearing at her heart. Wearing jeans or dress clothes, he made her heart rate increase. But he wore something else that had the opposite effect on her. The remembered gleam of the wedding ring on his third finger proclaimed the state of his heart.

"He's a distraction, Lord. If I didn't know better, I'd think he's showing an interest in me. But, even if he were, I couldn't return the interest. My life is on an even keel now. Or it was. I don't need a man in my life. That kind of relationship only leads to hurt. It's too big a risk. A quiet lifestyle is natural for me. No man would ever put me first in his heart and share his whole life with me."

Don't fret. Let me take care of you.

She opened her eyes and released a sigh of resignation. "Okay, Lord, you're the boss."

Haley picked up her oversized purse and dug out the jump rope she kept in it. Then she took it to the rear bedroom she had made into a den. Furnished sparsely with a sofa, desk and computer at one end and a small television near it, the rest of the floor space had been left clear. A rectangle of outdoor carpet lay on top of the regular rug. She stepped onto it and flipped the rope behind her back. Then she began to turn it and jump. Faster and faster she turned, letting the frenetic exercise consume her and block everything from her mind.

Exhausted after the workout, Haley took a shower and went to bed.

~

Friday morning Haley hit the floor and dressed with single-minded purpose. Refusing to allow anything to occupy her mind but her job, she went to work and was hiking along a block, Pistol at her side, when the dog stopped abruptly. His ears went up, and he whined. Then he went trotting across the lot to a small storage shed.

Curious, Haley stopped on the sidewalk and watched him disappear around the side of the shed. Moments later she heard him yip. Then banging and yelling came from inside the shed. It did not sound like children playing.

Following the path Pistol had taken, Haley had just reached the side of the shed when the dog barked again—and the banging and yelling increased. Alarmed, she rounded the building and found the dog pawing at the front door.

"What is it, boy?" She placed a hand on Pistol's head and peered through the small rectangular window above the door handle. Dennis was inside, wailing and beating on the door. Haley looked down at the piece of tree limb, one end anchored in the ground, the other pushed up against the door to brace it shut, trapping Dennis inside. Enraged, she kicked the stick away and jerked the door open.

Dennis ran out and threw his arms around her. "Thank you, Miss Mailman," he blubbered into her neck. Then he dropped to his knees and wrapped his arms around Pistol's neck. "Dennis can't get out," he sobbed.

Haley squatted next to the child. "How did Dennis get locked in there?"

He buried his face in the dog's neck, his body trembling. "Door not open."

Haley placed a hand on his shoulder. "Dennis, I need to know who locked you in there. Will you tell me?"

Dennis turned his face aside, still clutching the dog, and shaking his head. "No can tell you."

This child was afraid of someone. Who? The very idea made Haley so angry she could hardly think. She pulled her cell phone from her pocket and placed a call. "May I speak to Chief Richards?" she asked when deputy Collins answered.

He hesitated a second. "Haley?"

"Yes," she said through tight lips. "Dennis needs his grandpa."

"Tell me where you are, and I'll send him right there."

Haley gave him the location and disconnected. Then she put her bag down and sat on the ground beside the boy and dog. "Dennis, your grandpa is coming," she said quietly.

He hiccupped and peered around at her, almost furtively.

"Aren't you a little far from home?" She hoped he would talk to her and grow calmer.

His tongue protruded as he considered the question. Then his face crumpled again. "Dennis in trouble 'gin. Not 'sposed to leave the block."

"So why did you?" She wanted to comfort him, but once again Pistol seemed to have more ability to do that than she did.

Dennis drew a deep breath and grew quiet. Then he mumbled against the dog's neck. "Dennis wanted to see what they did."

Haley frowned. "What who did?"

He shook his head forcefully. "No can tell you."

"Do you see what other kids do in the neighborhood?"

He turned his head toward her and rolled his eyes upward. "Yeah."

Ah. "You mean the older kids?"

His head bobbed again.

She considered whether to broach the next line of thought. "Do the older kids ever go down and hang out around the funeral home?"

His eyes darted from side to side. "Sometimes."

"Do they ever play around back where the hearse is parked?"

This time he didn't speak, but after a long pause, he nodded.

Haley held her breath before the next question. "Do you know who scratched the hearse or broke the glass in the sign?"

His eyes grew big and round. "You know about that?"

She gave him a nod and what she hoped was a grin. "I know about that."

"Billy did it. He was mad." Dennis jerked his head

back around and hugged Pistol tighter.

Haley started to ask another question, but the arrival of a police car at the curb interrupted her. Chief Richards emerged and hurried across the yard to them.

"Thank you, Miss Haley," he said as he boosted Dennis to his feet. "I think I may have to deputize you or make you a neighborhood watch woman—or something along that line." He directed a tight smile over his grandson's head at her.

"Thanks, but I already have a job, and I'm running late on it." She pointed at the piece of tree limb. "The door was propped shut with that, with Dennis inside. He won't say who did it."

"We'll have a talk about it, maybe over an ice cream cone. Would that be all right?" he asked Dennis.

The boy's face brightened. "Yeah. Dennis like ice cream."

"Thanks again," the chief said as they walked to his car.

Haley shouldered her bag and headed up the street.

~

Haley slept like a baby that night—a very tired baby. Saturday morning she woke at her usual time, and then remembered that she didn't have to go to work. She eased out of bed, dressed in comfy jeans and tee shirt, and headed to the kitchen. At the end of the hall she paused to glance out the window, and came to a complete halt when she saw a black Cherokee parked at the edge of the yard. Neil sat slumped behind the wheel, sleeping. The passenger window was down a few inches for air to circulate. What in the world was he doing here?

Haley marched outside and tapped on the windshield. Neil shot upright, his eyes darting over at her.

"What are you doing out here?" she asked when he lowered the window a little more.

His face took on a sheepish look. "Would you believe sleeping?"

"That's obvious, but why here?"

He raked a hand over his face. "I couldn't sleep last night. After I finally did drop off, it didn't last. I woke up early and decided to come see if you'd like to go to breakfast with me. You weren't up yet, and I didn't want to wake you, so I decided to wait until I saw lights or some sign of life."

"And fell asleep," she finished for him with an exasperated shake of her head. "Well, if you're going to do such a silly thing, you may as well come in and let me feed you breakfast."

"My, my, how gracious," he mocked. A twitch at the corners of his mouth cancelled any sarcastic effect of the words. He flexed his shoulders and twisted his head, working out the kinks.

"But you'll take me up on it, huh?" She spun and went back to the house, fully conscious of him following behind her.

Inside the house, she turned to face him. "Would you prefer to eat now, or do you need to take a nap on the couch first? You said you didn't sleep last night, and I can imagine how much rest you got out there."

The look he gave her was studied. "You wouldn't mind if I slept awhile?"

She noted the darkness under his eyes. "It's only six o'clock. Why don't you crash while I work? I'll wake you when the food's ready."

He considered for a moment. "If I do, can we take a drive out to the lake after we eat?"

She hadn't bargained for an outing with him, but it seemed harmless enough—and altogether too tempting. "All right. How many eggs do you want?"

He grinned. "Two, over easy."

Haley found him a pillow while he removed his shoes.

Chapter 4

*N*eil woke to the smell of bacon and coffee. He rubbed a hand over his face and sat up. Through the doorway he could see Haley taking something from the refrigerator. "You wouldn't happen to have an extra toothbrush, would you?"

As soon as the words left his mouth, he realized how intimate they seemed. But he couldn't take them back. He needed to cool it. *Look after her, but keep things light, Bronson. Don't forget the lessons you've learned.*

She closed the refrigerator and came to the living room door. "There should be extra ones in the top right drawer of the bathroom vanity." She placed butter and jelly on the table. "The bathroom's the first door on the right up the hall."

After he brushed his teeth and washed his face, Neil felt better. Back in the dining room, Haley had the table set and was pouring milk and orange juice. He took the seat across the table from her.

There was an awkward moment of silence. "Would you like me to offer the blessing?"

She nodded. "Please."

They bowed their heads, and he spoke a few simple words of thanks for the food God had provided. "Did you visit your mother in the hospital yesterday?" she asked when they had their plates filled.

He nodded. "Yes. She got through the spinal surgery just fine, but she's facing months of rehab and more surgeries down the line. She's already had two knee replacements, and one of those needs redoing. What about your mother? Did you see her?"

"Yes. Nothing changes. She's well cared for, which is all I can ask."

"Where do you go to church these days?" he asked, and then feared he had been too abrupt in his change of subject.

She took her time answering. "Here and there," she admitted at last. "I went to South Side Bible with Mom and my sisters when we were kids, but I haven't been back there in a long time."

He remembered seeing her with her family, and sometimes with her three girlfriends. Looking back, he realized that Haley had insulated herself by keeping everyone at a distance. He thought he understood it now. She had felt looked down on and put up a thick wall to protect herself from the kind of hurtful put-downs that teens could so thoughtlessly inflict on anyone they perceived as a bit different. He could kick himself for being so blind at the time.

"I became a Christian when I was nine," she continued. "But I never grew a lot spiritually. After I left home I did better. I didn't attend regularly while I was in the military, but during the short time I worked in Springfield I attended a loving church where I felt welcome and accepted. I had started to get involved in some mission projects."

Neil silently interpreted her story. After Rick made her feel like a fool, she had fled their small town and gone looking for a better life. Good for her. He reached for another slice of bacon. "Now that you're back, where have you gone?"

She shrugged and also took a piece of meat. "I've been visiting around."

"My family still attends South Side Bible Church. I know they would welcome you back."

She split her biscuit in half and poured gravy over it, making no comment. He debated whether it was a good time to broach the subject of Teen College again. Considering that it started in less than two weeks, he felt it was necessary.

"I've extended my leave through the end of July so I can do Teen College for Dad. He has the Bible and missions study materials already on hand, but he thinks we should add a couple more electives."

Haley frowned and lowered the bite she had started to put in her mouth. "Electives?"

He put his fork down. "Vacation Bible School is structured with contained classrooms according to age, like in elementary school. But for Teen College the church does it more like high school. There are required classes—the Bible and mission studies—but then they each get to choose from a list of electives to round out their schedules. The beauty of it for workers is that they don't have to be there the whole evening, but just long enough to do their own classes."

A smile spread across her face. "Has it gotten more participation that way?"

"Dad says they've had much better attendance since they started this."

"What kind of extra electives do you have in mind?"

Good. He had her interested. "I think I'll offer a construction class."

Her mouth dropped open. "Construction?"

He grinned and nodded. "We'll build a scale model of heaven."

Her look turned speculative. "You mean figure out the dimensions and materials described in the Bible and build it on a table, kind of like in those movie scenes where military officers build models of battlefields?"

He nodded more vigorously. "We'll use foil, glass, marbles, pieces of old jewelry, I don't know what all, to represent the city of gold, jasper walls, and precious stones."

Seeing the glow in her face as she wrapped her brain around the idea made the planning all the more pleasurable. She captivated him, the only woman since Beth to do so. His resolve to keep this impersonal didn't seem to be working. An automatic smile crossed his face. "You could do a class on beauty."

She reacted instantly. "Oh, no. I know nothing about beauty treatments or products."

"But you know about inner beauty and what the Bible teaches about it. You could find a way to blend the outer and inner beauty concepts." The kind of deeper beauty he admired in her probably could not be taught, but the general idea from a biblical perspective could be presented.

A thoughtful look came over her face. "You mean like maybe have a cosmetologist come in and do a demonstration of the proper way to apply makeup, and follow it with a lesson on inner beauty?"

She had taken the bait. "Right. Will you do it?"

Haley hesitated, as if wavering, but then she relented. "I suppose I can. Kelsey Monroe would probably do the demonstration. How many lessons would I need?"

"Five," he said, being careful to keep his outward expression from revealing his inner satisfaction. "They'll meet Monday through Friday evenings. Regular Bible School meets the same week, but in the mornings. I told Chief Richards I'll see that his grandsons get there and back."

Haley eyed him with a grin that bordered on a grimace. "Let me guess. Dennis is excited about it, but Tommy not so much."

Neil nodded. "Sam says Tommy has to go. I don't

know that I like the idea of VBS being a punishment, but it's not my decision. I'm glad he'll be there, though."

"Punishment for what?" Haley asked before beginning to eat again.

"Sam convinced Dennis to admit who locked him in the storage shed."

She chewed silently, waiting for an explanation.

"The Chief stopped by the funeral home yesterday afternoon. He said Dennis forgot," he bracketed the word with his fingers, "to stay in his restricted area and followed Tommy to that shed where he and some more boys were smoking cigarettes. When Dennis told them he was going to tell on them, they caught him and locked him in the shed."

Haley's head moved back and forth. "It's too bad that Tommy isn't more caring and protective toward his little brother."

"The chief and his daughter are concerned about Tommy and the boys he's running with. They've agreed that Sam will see that he attends Bible School, and further discipline will be handled by Cindy."

"Did Dennis tell you or his grandpa that Billy damaged your hearse and sign?"

Neil grimaced. "Yeah, but he doesn't know Billy's last name. Or won't tell it." He concentrated on finishing the great breakfast she had fixed.

After they finished eating, he helped Haley clear the table and load the dishwasher. He found himself enjoying the domestic activity and wanting to spend even more time with her. But the last thing he needed was to get involved in the kind of relationship that could lead to marriage—and the possibility of pregnancy. His chest tightened, the pain between his ribs nearly unbearable. No way could he risk that.

~

"Is there a special reason for coming here?" Haley asked as Neil drove over the spillway.

Here was Bagnell Dam, which impounded the Lake of the Ozarks reservoir at its northeastern end. The lake itself snaked across four counties.

He glanced across the seat of the Cherokee at her. The wraparound sunglasses he wore looked good, but Haley regretted that they covered his eyes.

"I thought we'd run out to the park for a hike. I don't know about you, but I like to get out in the open spaces when I have decisions to make."

Haley assumed his decisions had to do with the care of his parents.

"The Chamber of Commerce asked me to help set off fireworks for their Fourth of July display."

"If you're getting involved with the Chamber, you must be considering staying around."

"I have to decide within a few more days whether to quit my job."

"If you do, will you continue to run the mortuary full-time?"

His mouth pulled up at one side. "I'm not sure what I should do."

He drove to the Lake of the Ozarks State Park and turned in at the entrance. Then he parked in the lot and turned to face her. "There's another matter that I've never shared with anyone other than Beth."

Haley didn't know what to think. Why would he tell her things he hadn't told his family and friends? Did it mean he felt comfortable enough talking to her to share his secrets? She didn't interrupt.

He draped an arm over the steering wheel and met her gaze. "I studied criminal justice and business management in college, but I took a lot of Bible and ministry classes as electives."

Bam. She hadn't expected that. "Are you saying you're considering the ministry?"

His eyes stayed locked on her. "I'm saying I'm wrestling with whether God is calling me to the ministry."

"Have you done any preaching?"

A cloud passed over his face. "Some. With Beth's encouragement, I filled in for my pastor a few times when he had to be gone. After that I began to do the same for a few other pastors, but I stopped when she died. I don't know if the feelings inside me are coming from guilt for that, or if God is truly leading me in that direction."

Oh, boy. That guaranteed that he had no serious interest in her. A failure at relationships, she could never handle being a pastor's wife. Not that such a role would ever be a possibility. Haley's rational side felt relief, but the other half of her knew disappointment that she would not be spending time with Neil beyond the Teen College commitment.

He heaved a deep breath and opened his door.

"Let's walk."

They met in front of the vehicle and hiked along one of the walking paths that wound through thousands of wooded acres. They were looping back around when two joggers appeared, coming toward them. Haley smiled when she recognized her friends from high school.

"Haley," Paige Kimball Taylor and Kelsey Monroe greeted her simultaneously and stopped to give her exuberant hugs. Paige taught music at the Ozark Christian Academy here at the lake, and Kelsey owned her own beauty salon in Skyview. The two of them, Haley, and Brooke Whitney had come out here often as girls.

"Hi, girls," Neil greeted them. "I see you two still like to keep fit."

Paige grinned good-naturedly and began to run in place, arms working back and forth. "We do. My hubby and kids are over past the pavilion." She jerked her head in that direction.

Haley knew an opportunity when she saw one. "Would you two be willing to help us with Teen College?" She launched into an explanation of the situation and what they had in mind.

"I'd love to do that," Kelsey responded, smiling when Haley finished outlining the beauty demonstration plans.

"I'll help in whatever way you need," Paige offered. "My family's going to barbecue after we finish our run. You two are welcome to join us."

Before either of them could respond, the sound of

a siren erupted from Neil's pocket. "Excuse me." He extracted a cell phone and answered it. He listened for several seconds, said, "I'll take care of it," and disconnected.

He faced Haley's friends. "We'll have to pass on the barbecue. Dad said the nursing home has had a death, and I need to make a pickup."

"Okay. Well, it was nice running into both of you." They both waved and jogged on down the path.

Without waiting for Neil, Haley headed for his truck.

"I'll drop you at home and keep moving," Neil said as they reached the city limits.

Haley gave him a sheepish look. "That sounds like a good idea."

"Are you afraid to ride around in a hearse with me?" He contorted his mouth into a vampire-like expression.

"I'll see you around." She opened the passenger door as he swung into her driveway.

When she entered the house, Haley wilted. Then, needing to clear her mind of silliness, she went to the den and grabbed her jump rope. How could she have let her emotions get tangled up with Neil Bronson?

Ten minutes later, exhausted from the additional workout, she tossed the rope over the back of the desk chair and collapsed onto the sofa. "Lord, I'm confused. Neil threatens my peace of mind. Don't let me fall for him again," she pleaded, squeezing the words through her constricted throat. "Help me stay sensible and trust You to guide my life."

She rolled over and stared up at the ceiling. She knew God heard her. But she didn't really expect an answer.

Although she had loved the church in Springfield, she had struggled since returning home. She believed that God loved her and *could* help her, but she lacked conviction that He *would*.

"Lord, all I do is beg for help constantly. Help Mom regain some use of her muscles. Help Dillon get his life on track. Help Leann become independent and not need me so much."

She stopped her agonized litany. Then she took a deep breath. "Lord, what do You want my life to be? What are You trying to tell me? What should I do?"

You are important to me. Trust me to show you the task I have for you.

She closed her eyes and let her body go lax. Ever so slowly, calmness crept over her. She rose and grabbed her purse. She needed to grocery shop.

~

Sunday morning Neil woke tired and groggy. It would have felt good to go back to sleep and skip church, but his conscience wouldn't let him do that.

Growing up, he had often protested about having to attend church. If left on his own, he would have slept in on Sunday mornings and hung out with friends on church nights. But his parents had taken him and Eric to services with them regularly. He had been involved in youth activities and mission organizations and attended summer Bible camp. He had become a

Christian at a young age, but had fallen into lazy habits after leaving home.

After his marriage to Beth, they had attended church with regularity and moved back to Skyview following his graduation from college. He had joined the police department and helped his dad at the mortuary when he could. During that time he had come to realize that God expected more of him than mere attendance at church. He had participated in mission projects and begun to accept requests for speaking engagements.

When Beth died, he had found himself, for the first time in his life, empty and angry, unable to speak God's word. Missing Beth's laughter and bright chatter, her sparkling eyes and blond curls, her enthusiasm for life—dying from grief—he had fallen to his knees and begged God for answers and comfort. No answers had been clear, but he had finally reached a point of acceptance. What he had not been able to bear was the pitying looks and careful treatment. He couldn't step into a pulpit.

He had resigned from the Skyview Police Department, gone to St. Louis, and taken the YMCA executive director position, needing complete change—or escape. New scenery. New people. New church. The combination had provided an environment where he could function without family and friends smothering him. He wasn't exactly healed. There would always be an empty hole in his heart, but at least now he could get up mornings and go about his life with a semblance of normality—and get a decent night's sleep.

Except last night. Why did Haley West intrude into his thoughts and disturb his sleep? She had always been cool and distant, a force unto herself, and only been close to Paige, Kelsey, and a girl named Brooke who spent summers with her grandmother and attendee church with her.

In the months after finding out the truth about Rick, Haley had literally built a wall around herself and become more reserved than ever. She had turned a blind eye to the opposite sex, making it clear she didn't need a boyfriend in her life, even if other girls thought having one was vital to their identity. No, Haley had focused on her studies and moved on, distancing herself emotionally and physically from those she felt looked down on her.

He couldn't blame her. The awareness, that protective instinct he had always felt toward her, had resumed as soon as he met her again. But he had all he could handle, running the business and taking over Teen College for his dad. After that, he might return to St. Louis and not see Haley any more. The thought brought an unexpected thrust of disappointment. It should make him happy, but it didn't. He wanted to spend more time with her, but he shouldn't. He didn't need the complication of a female relationship. That kind of thing led to entanglements, commitment, and heartbreak. He couldn't risk another marriage—or any subsequent pregnancy. Yet something about Haley made him question his resolves.

He pushed himself out of bed.

An hour later he sat in a pew next to his dad, Eric on the other side, without his wife. Jenny had stayed home with their sick baby, but insisted that Eric still attend with Dad.

Chapter 5

*H*aley questioned her sanity as she parked next to a stake at the end of the parking lot of South Side Bible Church. Yes, Neil had suggested she try attending it again. But now that she was here, she realized it might seem as if she were chasing after him. She entered the building and slipped into a back pew. Her heart quickened when she spotted his sturdy frame in a pew midway to the front of the auditorium.

She pulled her eyes away and focused on the empty pulpit. Moments later Kelsey slid onto the seat beside her and leaned over to whisper in her ear. "I'm so glad to see you here."

Haley hadn't kept in touch with her friends as

much as she should have, and they had respected her privacy and given her time to deal with her circumstances and grieving process, while letting her know they were always available if needed. Haley vowed that, from this point forward, she would connect with them more.

They went silent at the choir's entrance. The music service was uplifting, but the sermon seemed to be aimed directly at her.

"In God's mysterious way, His plan is for some Christian lives to be short. Our lives are in God's hands alone. Let's treasure our family and friends. Arguments happen. But let's make sure they are resolved. Grudges are a burden too heavy to carry. Focus more on living than dying."

As the pastor quoted from First Thessalonians, Haley's mind followed two tracks. On one she heard the words of the scripture—"*I do not want you to be ignorant, brethren, concerning those who have fallen asleep, lest you sorrow as others who have no hope.*" On the second track, her mortality stared her in the face.

Grief and anger had alienated her from her brother. She had to resolve that—while she still had time.

At the end of the service, there was an invitation for everyone to stay for the covered dish dinner being served in the fellowship hall.

"You are staying, aren't you?" Kelsey's expression was hopeful.

Haley shook her head. "I didn't know about it and

didn't bring a dish."

"Oh, pooh." Kelsey waved away her argument. "There's always enough food to feed an army, and everyone takes home at least half of what they brought. Please eat with us. I saw Ada Fisher come in with a vinegar pie, and Mrs. Holden brought one of her famous chocolate cream ones."

Haley rolled her eyes in defeat, knowing how relentless Kelsey could be. "And you won't touch it, of course." Her health conscious friend believed chocolate was harmful to her skin and was proud of the fact that she hadn't tasted any since her early teens.

Kelsey just smiled and led the way to the fellowship hall. After the blessing, they filled their plates, with Haley snagging a piece of the coveted chocolate pie rather than risk coming back later and finding it all gone. They got iced tea from the drinks counter and found a vacant table. They had just gotten settled when Haley spotted Neil and his dad and brother headed their way. She lowered her line of vision.

"May we join you?"

Even as Neil spoke, the three men slid their plates onto the table across from Haley and Kelsey, forcing Haley to look up. As usual, the sight of Neil took her breath away. Those riveting dark eyes seemed to drill right through her. It was a relief when the pastor and his wife joined them. Pastor Bill Callahan might be short and bald, but his manner was more lively and engaging than any older pastor Haley had ever met. He put his heaping plate down and smiled across the table at her. "It's good to have you join us, Haley. I see you around town, but I hardly recognize you out of uniform."

Haley grinned back at him, glad she had worn her favorite black dress with pink piping trim. "It feels good to wear something different on Sundays, but it's nice during the week to not have to worry about what to put on each day."

"She looks nice no matter what she wears," Kelsey interjected matter-of-factly. "I'm not happy about why she came home to live, but I'm thrilled she's here."

The pastor frowned, sympathy etching across his face. "I'm sorry for your loss. Your family has been on my prayer list ever since the accident."

"Thank you," was all Haley could say. She glanced away to maintain her composure, and found Neil's gaze focused on her.

"Do you remember Eric?" he asked.

Haley nodded. "Hello, Mr. Bronson. Eric. I've always known you from a distance, but never had the opportunity to get personally acquainted. I'm pleased to have that pleasure now."

As her eyes traveled from one to the other of the three Bronson men, she made note of their relaxed manner. They fit into this—or any—group so comfortably. The differences between her life and theirs stood out in her mind like a giant chasm. They were upstanding community and church leaders, at ease in any setting. She lacked those social skills.

She tried to relax, and focused on the elder

Bronson. "I hope your wife is doing well."

He paused in the act of drizzling sweetener from a pink packet into his iced tea. His hair might be steel gray, but it still curled around his head in thick array. "She's in good hands, but I need to be with her."

He turned to the pastor. "Why are those stakes in the parking lot?"

The pastor's smile morphed into a troubled frown. "We have a serious problem. I spent Thursday morning in Jefferson City making hospital visits and seeing my own doctor. When I returned to town, I noticed the stakes and asked about them. No one I asked had any idea why they were there. That afternoon the school superintendent called and informed me that the church doesn't own the area we've been parking on since the church was built in 1942."

Collective gasps of dismay sounded around the table.

"How can that be?" Neil asked, shock making his question sharp.

The pastor shook his head. "I don't know how it happened, but an error was made in the survey way back then and never caught. The only reason it came to light now is because the school had to have their property surveyed before they can sell it."

Expressions said that everyone understood that part, but they were still in disbelief about the error. The school district had constructed a new elementary building over the past two years across town near the high school. This summer they had moved everything but old equipment and furnishings they no longer wanted to use into the new structure.

Haley had followed the progress and heard talk about what the district planned to do with the old building, but it had only recently been publicly announced that the property would be sold. This development could not have been foreseen.

"How much property is at stake?" she asked.

"The school's property line extends across the access road and half of our parking lot," the pastor answered, his mouth exhibiting a slight tremor.

Silence fell as the implications sank in.

"What can we do?" Haley's face heated as she realized she had said we. It astonished her that she had identified with these people so quickly.

The pastor faced her, but his words were for everyone. "I requested that the superintendent put the church on the agenda for the school board meeting."

"When will it be?" Neil asked.

"The tenth of July. That's on a Tuesday. I hope several members will attend."

Nods came from those present.

The pastor cleared his throat. "Friday morning our local news reporter, Darlene Fowler, came to the office and asked what we intend to do about our property line dispute. When I didn't immediately tell her any plans, she seemed to take delight in explaining to me how the school is going to sell the old building and property, including what the church thought was theirs. According to her, it sounds like a done deal, and we'll no longer be able to use the access road. "We'll have to make a road of part of our existing parking lot, and we don't have enough room to build more parking lot space."

He had managed to keep his tone steady, but Haley could tell how troubled he was by his eyes and body language. "My neighbor works at the courthouse. If you have no objection, I'll ask him to get us a copy of the survey records. It can't hurt to double check."

"I'd appreciate that," the pastor said.

Neil's gaze zeroed in on her. "Why don't you and I measure the lot after you get the survey records? Will you call me as soon as you have the information?"

"I can do that."

Pastor Bill's eyes brightened. "Thank you both for your help."

His wife leaned forward. "Haley, are you the one we should also be thanking for helping Mrs. Kirkpatrick?" She referred to an elderly church member.

Haley shook her head. "I didn't help her personally. I just reported that her mail hadn't been picked up in a couple of days and I hadn't seen her."

"Well, I believe that saved her life," the tiny woman insisted. "A deputy checked on her, found her unconscious, and called an ambulance."

"Her air conditioner had quit, and she got too hot," Haley explained. "Do you know how she's doing?"

"She's much better."

The pastor spoke again. "I called a repairman to fix her air conditioner. The church will pay for it, since she's alone and living on a small fixed income. She's been a blessing to others over the years. Now it's time for others to look after her."

Haley nodded agreement. "I'm happy to hear that."

"What about you?" Neil asked. "Are you slowing down and keeping hydrated in this extreme heat?"

Haley made a little laugh. "I pace myself and drink a lot of water, but others take care of me, too. When I deliver mail at the restaurant, they always have a cup of ice water for me. Then several citizens along the route meet me at the door with bottles of water."

"I'm glad to hear that."

Jim Bronson took a swig of tea, put his glass down, and faced Neil. "Have you met with the McKinley family yet?"

Neil nodded. "They came in last night and made arrangements. They're the family of the lady who died at the nursing home yesterday," he explained to Haley.

He turned his attention back to his dad. "They asked me to conduct the service for them since their pastor is out of town."

Jim Bronson's eyes brightened. "Did you agree to do it?"

"I told them I would." Neil spoke slowly, as if afraid he had committed to something he shouldn't have.

Satisfied, Mr. Bronson tackled his food. Eating precluded more conversation.

Haley tried to picture Neil as a minister—without a wife to work alongside him. Quickly she banished the image.

A few minutes later, Mr. Bronson gathered his empty plate and stood. "I'm going to the hospital to see Lillian. I'll see you boys later."

Neil gave him a wave. "We'll be there in a half hour or so."

~

Neil sat in an uncomfortable metal chair next to his brother, facing their dad across their mother's hospital bed. Dad looked tired, his hair rumpled and his eyes clouded. After a visit with her doctor, Mom had fallen asleep. Doctor Thomas had told them he wanted to move her to the nursing home for rehab, predicting that it could be a long recovery.

The antiseptic smells, blended with the discouragement in his dad's face and the floral arrangements around the room, sent weakness sweeping over Neil. It hurt to see his mother's frail body and wan face there in the bed. It hurt to see his dad suffering. The knot in his throat tightened until he could hardly breathe.

"Dad, why don't you go home and get some rest? I'll stay here."

"So will I," came from Eric.

Jim shook his head. "I want to be here when she wakes up, and spend as much time with her as I can."

"She may sleep a long time," Neil pointed out. "Promise you'll go home at a decent hour."

"I'll be fine," he said without making any promise. He ran a hand over his face, as if raking away his fatigue. "You boys go on. I'm sure you have business you need to take care of."

Neil faced Eric. "You have a sick kid. Go home and check on her."

Dad rose and came around the bed. "I'll walk you both out." Once in the hallway, he only went as far as the waiting room and sank onto the brown leather sofa. He pointed at the chairs facing him and indicated they should sit. Then he faced them, his eyes glistening. The fingers of his right hand caressed the gold wedding band on his left ring finger.

"This situation is never going to get better," he said, his chin wobbling in spite of his effort at control. "Your mom has had so many surgeries already, and there will be more. The disease is all through her now. I'm going to put the business up for sale."

Neil and Eric both started to speak, but Jim raised a silencing hand. "Lillian can't work anymore, and I need to be with her. I know neither of you boys really wants to run the mortuary. And don't you dare feel guilty about it." He waggled a finger at them.

Neil did feel guilty, though, and he knew Eric shared his regret at their lack of desire to carry on the business where their parents had worked, and then owned, for so many years. Mom and Dad considered it a ministry to help people in their times of grief.

Dad directed his next words at Eric. "You have a nice family and a job that means a lot to this community. I'm proud of you."

Next he addressed Neil. "Son, we understood when you left that you needed to get away from the many reminders of your loss here. We've prayed and prayed for you. I'm happy you're finally able to get on with your life, and I don't want you to give up your job and come back here to take care of a business that doesn't really appeal to you. If you can stay through your scheduled leave, I'll be able to manage better with Lillian in the nursing home."

Yes, he would manage, but it would take a toll on him, even for whatever amount of time it took to find a buyer for the business. Neil could see what all this had already done to him. Pain squeezed his heart.

Dad's expression lightened a bit. "I noticed a certain spark in your eyes at lunch. It's good to see you showing interest in a gal."

"He's always had a soft spot for Haley," Eric interjected before Neil could deny anything.

Neil glared at his older brother. "I admire and respect her. Always did. But that's all."

Eric's smile dimmed a bit, but he didn't back off. "Maybe it's time for you to at least admit you like her."

Neil couldn't deny that. He hadn't realized how much attention Eric had paid to him in the past. Just how much did he know?

It was a relief when Dad pushed to his feet. "I'm going back to Lillian. I just wanted to let you boys know my plans."

They watched him walk away. Then Neil faced Eric. "I may move back permanently."

Eric studied him. "From guilt, or responsibility, or because it's what you really want?"

Neil took a deep breath. "It may be time to come

home. Dad needs help, no matter what he says. And the community seems to be drawing me into it."

"I'd love to have you back—all of us would—but don't come just because you feel obligated. Of course, if there's a more personal attraction, that would be fine." Eric's mouth twitched.

Neil took his time responding. "I don't know. She's a friend, and she's easy to talk to."

"That's good. You're lonely, and she's a sweet person. I think Beth would approve, if that's holding you back."

"I'm not sure I'm ready to move on in that way." Neil gave him a wry look. "But I'm glad you approve."

As if having exchanged a mental command, they stood and went their separate ways.

Chapter 6

*H*aley's shoulders sagged. The meal at the church, as well as the visit with Kelsey, had been pleasant. Seeing Neil again had also been nice. Too nice. She had no business crying for the moon—or having anything to do with men. Rick had taught her that. And she had seen the imbalance of her parents' relationship, with her mother carrying so much of the load.

Unwilling to settle for such an unequal partnership, Haley preferred to channel her energies into her work. She couldn't get derailed now. Meeting Neil, even for something as innocent as measuring the church parking lot, could do just that. But she cared about the church's plight and had agreed to help look for answers.

"Lord, why does it have to be like this? I don't understand."

She called her neighbor and explained what she needed.

"Can you come by the courthouse right after work?" he asked when she finished. "I'll have it ready for you."

"I finish my route about four-thirty. If I head straight there, I should make it by five o'clock."

"I'll wait for you if you're not there, since I know you'll be on your way."

She brushed her teeth and went to bed, not bothering with her usual session with the jump rope.

Monday morning Haley showered and crawled into a uniform. She walked through the back door of the post office promptly at seven-thirty and tossed her purse into a space near the mail cubbyholes.

"Morning, Haley." Vince smiled at her from his desk.

"Morning," she returned, grabbing her time card and shoving it into the clock.

As it clicked and she pulled it out, Brad entered through the back door and grabbed the key to a truck from a cubbyhole. "Ready to go?"

"Yep." She snagged a key to the other truck, and they went out together to inspect the trucks. Brad backed one up to the dock while she watched and looked it over. Then he inspected hers. Finished, they went inside and began to sort the mail that had arrived earlier that morning.

When that was done, Haley bundled envelopes by delivery loops and loaded everything into her truck. She returned the empty containers, grabbed her scanner, and returned to the truck.

As she slid behind the wheel, a helmet-wearing biker came zipping around the building and roared past her. Haley couldn't be sure, but she thought she recognized the oldest Fowler boy, Darlene's son.

At the street corner she turned left onto Main Street, proceeded up the block, and parked next to a building that currently housed a flea market. She exited, locked the truck, and headed north with her bag on her shoulder.

Haley worked her way up the block, delivering mail at each business or residence. At the end of the second block she crossed the street and stepped inside the funeral home foyer, hoping she would not run into Neil. She had lain awake last night, reproaching herself for being so friendly with him. How could she have forgotten how he really felt about her? It was just his nature to take care of others.

Not seeing him, but hearing sounds coming from a back room, Haley placed the mail on the small table beside the door and exited like a rabbit on the run. As she walked along the sidewalk, her resentment continued to fester. She should have avoided him.

When she finished the downtown loop, ending up back at the truck, Haley drove to the north end of town, parked in her usual spot, and took off walking.

Pleased with the time she was making, she rounded a corner and headed up a street bordered by a high wooden privacy fence. She had reached the middle of the block when voices carried from the other side of it.

Haley paid only cursory attention—until a phrase jolted her into awareness.

" ...dumb kids and their stupid gang ..." The sneering words came from a young voice.

Haley slowed her pace and listened more closely.

" ...was so funny." The second voice could hardly be heard.

"Yeah," the first voice said. "That funny kid ...did you see how scared he was?"

The second one laughed. " ...a riot ...won't tell anything so long as we got the kid."

Dennis? Got the kid? Had something happened to Dennis?

Haley broke into a run. At the end of the block she rounded the corner of the fence and raced to the gate about twenty-five yards away. She shoved it open and stepped inside the Clifford's back yard. No one was there, but she spotted movement beyond the small frame house next door.

Two bicycles shot from the other side of the house and went flying down the street. Only able to see the backs of their heads, Haley didn't recognize the boys, and there was no way she could catch them. She pulled out her cell phone and rang the police station.

"Is Dennis all right?" she blurted as soon as someone answered.

"He's fine," Chief Richards answered. "Is this Haley?"

"Yes," she said on a whoosh of relief.

"I just left Dennis a few minutes ago. What's wrong?"

Haley gave him a rushed explanation of what she had heard.

An audible sigh came across the line. "I don't know what's going on, but the neighborhood kids seem overly restless this summer. I'll call the babysitter to be sure Dennis is where he's supposed to be, and tonight I'll see if I can get Tommy to tell me anything. Thanks for calling."

Haley disconnected and looked around, still bothered. This small house belonged to the church beside it. They no longer used it as a parsonage, having upgraded to a better place a couple of blocks up the street. In poor shape, the little building was used by the congregation for storage.

Curious, Haley walked up onto the front porch and peered through the window. Stacks of storage boxes lined the walls, and a low table sat in the middle of a littered room. It looked like someone—kids?—had been hanging out in there.

She worked her way around the house, peeking inside all the windows. An odd variety of items filled each room—a Christmas tree and assorted Christmas items. More stacks of boxes. The living room appeared to be the only room that had been disturbed.

Haley made a mental note to ask the pastor when she saw him if he knew that their vacant parsonage was being used as a hangout by the neighborhood kids.

She returned to her route and finished the loop.

Then she drove to her usual parking spot on the west side of town to begin the five-hour trek there. As she climbed out of the truck, a black Cherokee drove up the street and parked behind her. She had to pull a deep stabilizing breath when Neil emerged and came striding toward her.

Haley fought a conflict of emotions. She didn't want to talk to him, but he looked better every time she saw him. There wasn't an iota of fat on his muscular frame. His mouth was firm, his eyes deep set. He wore jeans and a white shirt. She ignored him and headed up the street.

"Hey, where's the fire?" he asked as he caught up to her.

She didn't look at him or slow down. "I have to stay on schedule."

"Why the cold shoulder?" he demanded as she hiked across the railroad tracks.

Haley's jaw clenched. She stopped and faced him. Having nursed her resentment for years, an unreasonable anger bubbled in her. "You're such a fine, upstanding citizen, raised by a family of respected community leaders. Aren't you afraid of being seen out in public with one of that poor West bunch?"

She clamped her mouth shut, shocked that the long buried thoughts had actually spewed out of her mouth. She spun and took off.

"Whoa." A hand on her forearm stopped her. "Where did that come from?"

Haley couldn't prevent a grimace at the pain from the tight grip. He looked down at his hand and quickly withdrew it. "Sorry. I didn't mean to hurt you. But I do want an answer."

Haley took a deep breath, wanting to run. All the old unresolved feelings welled to the surface. She didn't know how to deal with them. Never had. She had run from everything—the town, her family, Neil—as soon as she finished high school. She had known when he got married, when his wife died, and when he left Skyview. So when her family needed her so desperately, it had seemed safe to return.

His return had thrown her into an instant tailspin. She gave him a helpless stare.

His somber study of her made Haley drop her eyes. He had aged and matured over the past ten years, but his adulthood was more compelling than his youthful attraction, even as those intense dark eyes she remembered so well bored into her and reduced her to jelly.

"What have I ever done to warrant being accused of looking down on you? Which is what that sounded like." His deep voice vibrated with impatience.

"I'm sorry," she said in a hoarse whisper. "I shouldn't have said it."

"But something triggered it. What happened? Be honest with me."

She raised her eyes. As she did, a passing van honked. She glanced over just in time to recognize Mrs. Mohler waving at them. She waved back. Great. Arguing with Neil on the street of a small town was as good as taking out a full-page ad in the paper.

Knowing he expected an answer, she firmed her

stance. "Back in high school I heard you and your friends talking one day when you didn't know I was nearby. One of the girls made a nasty crack about that West bunch, and you went along with it."

He went still, his eyes making a rapid movement under furrowed brows. "Somebody made a crack about your family, and you think I supported it."

She nodded, her mouth gone dry. She hitched the slipping strap of the mailbag back up onto her shoulder.

He exhaled slowly. "I think I might remember the incident you mean. But I didn't agree. I just didn't disagree. I saw no point in arguing with narrow minded, jealous girls."

She frowned. "Jealous?"

His face scrunched into an expression that reminded her of a jack-o-lantern. "Of course. They may have had more money and possessions, but you had good grades, character, and the respect of the teachers."

Haley's eyes rounded in surprise at his unexpected words. Her mouth opened and closed.

His mouth quirked. "You were too insecure to know that, right?"

She nodded, still speechless. Then she turned and hastened on down the sidewalk, with him keeping pace.

She peeked back at the mail truck behind them. That truck—her job—represented physical security. Emotional security had so far eluded her.

She took a long slow breath and kept walking.

"You seem to know a lot about me. I mean other than what a fool Rick made of me." Why had she brought up that painful subject?

"I may have been two years ahead of you in school, but we both grew up here and knew everyone in our school. Rick may have hurt you, but you shouldn't let one mistake keep you from living life to the fullest."

His words brought the past rushing back. Rick Montgomery had been a senior, a star athlete and very popular with the girls, when Haley was a lowly sophomore. When he started paying attention to her, she had been intimidated at first. But it hadn't taken long for her to respond like any young, vulnerable girl would do. She became infatuated with him and started meeting him after games, interpreting the solitude of their meetings as a romantic secret rather than the clandestine assignations they really were. Her awakening and disillusionment had come at his funeral.

Two days after his graduation, Rick had been killed in a motorcycle accident. Haley had gone to the funeral and slipped into a back pew. Darlene Fowler, also a graduating senior and the daughter of a wealthy businessman, had become hysterical and wailed that she might be having Rick's baby and that they had planned to marry later that summer. Haley had not known they were considered a steady couple.

Two days later Neil had slid onto the bench next to Haley at a baseball game and told her that he knew about her and Rick and that she shouldn't let the bad experience damage her. His words and manner had been comforting, yet shocking. When she asked him if anyone else knew, he assured her that he didn't think so. He explained that he only knew because when he had seen Rick meet her after a game one day and asked him about it, Rick had admitted to liking her and meeting her without Darlene's knowledge.

Haley had died inside and locked her feelings behind a silent wall. Finding out she was the "other woman" had been devastating to her already fragile self-esteem. Over the years she had wondered if Darlene's coldness to her came from the fact that she had known—or at least suspected. Haley had determined never to be that vulnerable again, and had driven herself more than ever to achieve.

"Rick was a teenage error in judgment," she said stiffly. "I can't speak ill of the dead, so I'll just say that I got an education. I learned from my mistake and became a lot more careful about the people I trust. Subject now closed." She headed on up the hill to where Pistol waited, Neil still pacing her.

"Is Trooper Luke's dog still escorting the mail carriers?" he asked as they neared the intersection.

"Of course."

"I used to get a kick out of seeing him escort the guys when I would be out on patrol. I sometimes wondered if his loyalty to the mail carriers is because his owner wears a uniform."

Haley tipped her head in thought. "Hm. I hadn't considered it in that light."

"Does he ever miss a day?"

"Nope." Haley reached down and gave the dog an affectionate rub on the head. "He's a very smart dog, but he just doesn't get Sundays. Residents say he waits every day, seven days a week. On Sundays he waits a long time. When no one comes, he eventually goes home."

"You have to be in better shape than an athlete," he commented, changing the subject.

Haley straightened and faced Neil in exasperation. "I know you didn't come out here to talk about the past, or about Pistol. So why are you here?"

He hesitated, as if stricken with uncertainty. "Well, I knew about what time you reach that intersection each day, and I wanted to ask if you would go to the fireworks display with me. But you gave me a fireworks display of your own, and the conversation got so sparkling that I forgot." He gave her a grin that started out meek, but turned cheeky.

Taken off guard, Haley flushed with embarrassment. "Sorry about that."

He became serious. "Will you?"

She gave him a sheepish look. "After the way I talked to you, I'm surprised you would still ask. The holiday is Wednesday. What about church?"

"Services will be over long before dark, if they don't cancel. I'll call you after I check the schedules."

"Oh," she said, suddenly remembering something else. "I called my neighbor, and I'm going to the courthouse right after work today."

"I'll take you. That way we can come back by the church and measure the lot."

As she nodded agreement, a police car rolled past them. A boy glared at them through the window of the back seat.

"That's Ricky Fowler."

He nodded. "You mean Darlene and Rick's son. It appears they're arresting them younger every day." He spoke in what sounded like a weak effort to lighten the mood before turning and heading back to his Cherokee. "I'll be in touch."

Haley finished her route and headed back to the post office. She parked at the dock, took everything inside, and then came back out and moved the truck to the rear of the lot. Back inside, she punched the time clock to separate office and street time, emptied the trays, deposited the outgoing mail she had picked up, and separated the rest of the pile into letters, flats, and parcels. She turned in her keys and accountables—certified letters, delivery receipts, anything for which she had signed. After putting up empty equipment and sorting undeliverable mail, she clocked out and left the building.

Chapter 7

*N*eil sat in his Cherokee, watching the back door of the post office for Haley to emerge. With the motor still running, he upped the air conditioning. How did Haley walk all those miles in this heat?

Her well-being isn't your concern.

"She's just a friend," he reminded himself.

Yeah, a friend who would run the other way if he showed any interest in her beyond friendship, which could not happen anyhow. He had loved Beth and lost her. He couldn't deal with anything like that again.

Well, he didn't have to worry about anything serious developing between him and Haley. He was a reminder of times she wanted to forget.

So why did he have such a persistent compulsion to seek her out?

What would you do if something happened to her?

He swiped a hand across his brow at the thought. Such a question should only occur if they had a serious relationship. Yet an empty feeling came over him at the prospect of not seeing her any more. Did he really think he could make her life better?

Yeah, pig brains.

Had he been able to help Beth? No.

Did he have a subconscious need to feel needed? Maybe.

In an effort to sort through his thoughts and emotions, he forced his mind back to the present situation. He had stopped by the police station to ask Sam Richards if he had found out Billy's last name yet. Sam hadn't, but he did mention bringing in the Fowler kid. Neil wanted to share that bit of information with Haley. As she came out the back door, he gave his horn a brief tap.

When she looked up and veered toward the Cherokee, he leaned over and pushed the passenger door open. "You ready to go?"

She slid into the seat and placed her cap by her feet. Then she ran her hands through her sweat-moistened hair to loosen it from its flattened condition. "I should go home for a shower and shampoo, but there's no time."

"You look fine," he assured her. Of course, she always looked fine to him.

She rolled her eyes. "Yeah, for a street walker

who's been in the heat and dust all day."

He chuckled. "Don't be hard on yourself. You do a tough job and don't look bedraggled. By the way, I called the church secretary. Services will be held an hour earlier Wednesday night to allow more time for people to go watch the fireworks afterward. We can attend together and go from there to the lake."

When they entered the surveyor's office at the courthouse, a man greeted them and placed a folded sheaf of papers on the counter. "Hello, Haley. I made a copy of what you wanted."

"Can you also tell me what the value of that strip of land would be?" Neil asked the sparse-haired man whose nametag said Harry Ingram.

Harry darted a discreet glance at the clock. "I can do that." He pulled up a file on his computer and jotted some figures on a notepad. Then he tore off the top sheet and handed it to Neil. "Here you go."

Neil glanced at it. "I know it's late, but may I have a few more minutes to do some research?"

Harry nodded. " I'll wait as long as you need. Haley told me your problem," he added with a sympathetic smile.

Neil made good use of the time. When he finished, he returned to the front of the room. "Thanks for your help, and for waiting for us. We'll go now so you can do the same."

Harry smiled and began to shut down the computer. "Glad I could help. Stay cool," he cautioned Haley as they went out the door.

Haley studied the notes as Neil pulled out onto the

highway. He was sure he saw a comic-strip bubble filled with question marks form over her head.

"I did some recent sale comparisons so I could get an idea about how much vacant property is worth," he explained.

Her eyes lit with approval. "I studied the survey while you were doing that. The strip in question is more like a long wedge. We'll have to figure the value by footage rather than acreage." Her expression turned grave. "How could the church get into such a situation?"

His mouth tightened. "I've been asking people that all day. Apparently a mistake was made way back around the time the church was built. But since the church and school both used the access road and assumed they each owned the property on their side of it, no one ever challenged it. If the school hadn't decided to dispose of their property, the mistake wouldn't have come to light, at least for many more years."

"The church can't lose their parking space." A mixture of frustration and underlying anger laced the statement.

"God will provide a solution."

She studied him across the seat. "Are you sure?"

"I believe so. I've been praying about it, and I have a sense of calm."

She leaned back in the seat with a sigh. "I hope you're receiving the right message."

They didn't talk much for the rest of the ride. He pulled onto the church parking lot and took a tape measure and small notepad from the console.

"Hold the end of that," he instructed at the northernmost survey stake. Haley held it in place while he paced backward to the next stake. Following the survey map, they measured each property line and figured the total footage.

"According to the figures Harry gave me, this strip is worth about two thousand dollars," Neil said when he finished his calculations. "I'll visit with Pastor Bill tomorrow and see if he's ready to bring the matter to the church body. Are you too tired to go to the nursing home with me? I'd like to see if my mother has been admitted yet. You can visit your mother, and then we can go get something to eat."

She glanced down at her clothes. "I'm still in uniform."

"And look fine in it." She looked tired, but truly fine—and she had to have food.

She gnawed at her lower lip in indecision.

He pushed his advantage. "Don't make me wait until Wednesday night to fill you in on Ricky and the police."

She still hesitated, and he knew she was wrestling with whether she wanted to stretch the bounds of their friendship. "I don't think that's a good idea," she said at last.

He raked a hand through his hair. "It's just a meal."

She emitted a sigh of longsuffering. "Oh, all right."

He felt a rush of triumph, even if her agreement wasn't exactly gracious, not sure why it had become so important to pursue her this way. "Good. I'll take you back to the post office to get your wheels later."

She slid back into his Cherokee. At the nursing home, he stopped at the front office and stuck his head inside the doorway to ask if his mother had been checked in yet.

"I'll go on and see Mom." Haley continued on down the hall. He understood. She didn't want to intrude in his business, and she was anxious to see her own mother.

"The ambulance just arrived with her," the gray haired director said as he hung up the phone moments later. "It'll be awhile before we can get her admitted and ready for company."

Neil thanked the man and set off after Haley. He spotted her turning into a room near the far end of the hall. He walked to it and started to go inside, but came to an abrupt halt.

Haley stood immobile in the middle of the room, staring at the bed where her mother slept. A man sat in a chair next to her bed, his head lying on his folded arms. His shoulders shook, and choking sounds came from him.

Neil eased back to the edge of the doorway. He didn't want to intrude, but he couldn't bring himself to leave.

~

Haley remained frozen at the sight of her fragile mother lying there asleep, while her brother sobbed at the foot of her bed. So much hurt and grief. And it was all so needless. She clenched both fists and cried out in silent pain.

Why, God? Why did we have to end up like this? Please help us.

She couldn't prevent the sob that strangled her.

Dillon raised a ravaged face. His sandy brown hair was still worn in a short military cut, his brown eyes red rimmed. "I never meant to hurt 'em," he said in a shallow, thick voice.

"I know," she whispered in a voice just as strained. She bit down on her bottom lip to steady it. Neither of them liked to show emotion. They had been close as kids. Dillon had loved to tease her, his eyes sparkling with mischief. Now all she saw in those brown orbs was pain.

"I don't blame you for hating me," he croaked.

Tears flowed down Haley's cheeks. She had been so angry with him for letting alcohol ruin his own life, and in the process ending their sister's and damaging their mother's. She had never contacted him during the months he had been in prison, time that had to have been terrible for him. But she should have. He was her brother, and he had paid a huge price for his mistakes. He could never bring Reba back, or heal their mother's mind and body. But he had to go on living. Just like she did.

She moved toward him, unsure whether he would let her touch him. "I don't hate you," she said brokenly. "I'm sorry. I should have written you, or called."

He shook his head. "You had your hands full. I understand. I'm sorry I caused you to have to come back here and take care of everything—and everyone."

"It's okay." She rounded the end of the bed and knelt before him. When his bleary eyes met hers, she wrapped her arms around him. "You're my brother, Dillon. I love you."

He pulled her to him. "I let you down. Can you forgive me?"

She nodded and spoke into his chest. "I can. I know Mom already has. And I know God will if you ask Him."

He went still, but he didn't release her.

Haley pulled back enough to look into his face. "Mom always loved you so much. The thing that troubled her most was that, when Dad stopped going to church with her, you stayed home with him."

Dillon drew a slow breath and spoke, his voice nasal from crying. "That was wrong. Then there were more mistakes. I ran with the wrong guys and started drinking. While I was in the military I got worse. By the time I mustered out and came home, I was an alcoholic. And the ... " He broke off, unable to finish, and swiped at his eyes.

Haley reached up and stroked his face. "I know. You don't need to say any more."

He stood, pulling Haley to her feet with him. Her chin came even with his neck. He tipped her face up and looked straight into her eyes. "I'm sober now. I haven't had a drink since the accident. I know it's too little too late, but I hope I can make up for it in some small way. I know you've been taking care of things. Leann's written me a few times, so I know she finished high school and is starting college. That's good."

Haley knew he had to be broke, but he would refuse money if she offered it. "Do you have a place to stay?"

He shrugged. "I just got my freedom yesterday and arrived here about noon today. I called Justin Crandall, and he came after me in my old truck. I'm okay."

The little house where they had grown up had been sold to pay nursing home bills, so he had no place to go.

"Why don't you stay at my place for a while? I have a spare bed." Leann had stayed in it until she moved to Springfield.

He shook his head. "I know where you live. But you don't have to take care of me."

"I wish you would."

They both swiveled their heads around when the voice came from the doorway. Neil stepped into the room. How long had he been there? At least long enough to hear her invitation to Dillon. Had he been there during the whole conversation? The look of compassion on his face made Haley conclude that he had.

He crossed the room and extended a hand. "Good to see you, Dillon. God must have been in the timing of your arrival. Haley needs someone to help her look after things."

"Dillon?"

Mom's voice from the bed drew their attention. Head raised slightly off the pillow, her eyes darted back and forth in confusion.

"It's me, Mom," Dillon said gruffly.

Her mouth worked into a crooked smile, and her arms came up. "My boy."

Haley pressed a hand over her quivering mouth as Dillon leaned over and wrapped his arms around their mother. The knot in her windpipe made her gasp for breath.

For a long moment mother and son stayed in the embrace. Then Dillon drew back and made another swipe at his eyes. He sat on the edge of the bed and took his mother's hand. "I love you, Mom."

She produced a crooked smile and nodded in contentment. Then, ever so slowly, her eyes drooped and closed. The look on her face became peaceful as her chest rose and fell in sleep.

"She's had a cold, and they've been giving her antibiotics," Haley explained. "Seeing you will make her sleep better."

Satisfied that she was resting, Dillon freed his hand and rose. Together the three of them left the room.

"Do you still like to crawl under vehicles and see what makes them tick?" Neil asked Dillon, catching up with him as he made for the door.

"Sure," he answered without stopping. Haley followed them outside into the still hot, darkening air. Dillon stopped under the awning and faced Neil. "Why?"

"Eric mentioned Sunday that the school's bus mechanic is retiring in a few weeks. If you're planning to stick around and look for a job, you should drop by and fill out an application. Use me as a reference."

Surprise spread across Dillon's face. "Thanks. I just might do that."

"Haley and I are going to get something to eat. Why don't you join us?"

He shook his head. "Nah. I need to run to Wal-Mart and pick up a few things. But thanks for the invite." He loped off across the parking lot. Haley watched him get into the old red Ranger pickup he had bought back during his teens and could never afford to replace.

She faced Neil. "That was considerate of you. And trusting. Do you think the school will reject him because of his record?"

"Considering the nature of the offense, I don't think so. He wouldn't be considered a risk to others, and that job wouldn't have him driving the vehicles, only working on them. They like to keep hometown people around."

Haley looked back at the building they had just exited. "Isn't your mom here?"

"She was just arriving but hadn't been admitted yet when we got here. She won't care what time I visit, and I'm hungry. Let's go eat, and I'll come back."

In wordless agreement they headed for the Cherokee. Neil drove to the south end of town and swung into the parking lot of the local steakhouse. Inside, they found an empty table near the center of the room. Haley took off her uniform cap and placed it on the corner of the table. A waitress approached, pad and pen poised, and placed menus before them. "What would you like to drink?"

"Iced tea for me," Haley said. "And I'll have the shrimp platter."

Neil glanced at the menu and placed it back on the table. "Sounds good. Same for me."

When the waitress was gone, Haley aimed a serious look across the table. An unspoken connection arced between them, making it hard for her to speak. "It's not wise for us to spend so much time together, time that could be spent with your parents."

"Dad stays with Mom most of the time, and we have people who answer the phone and look after the business. Eric has his own family. That leaves me with plenty of time to spend as I please. So why shouldn't I spend some of it with you?"

"First of all, you may go back to St. Louis to live soon. And you feel guilty about being with me," she accused softly, directing a meaningful look at his left ring finger with the gold band around it.

Even as she said the words, Haley knew she wanted to seize every opportunity to be with him. But the cautious part of her was growing more afraid of the hurt she saw ahead.

His features tightened. "You're right, but it doesn't seem to matter. I don't know what God's plan is for us. It may just be a stronger friendship than before. Or it may be more. I'm beginning to feel like that's the case. How would you feel about that?"

She attempted to speak, but produced no sound.

"Let's just let God lead us," he said quietly. Then he changed the subject. "Dad informed Eric and me yesterday that he intends to put the business up for sale."

The waitress arrived with their drinks and salads. "Here you go. Is there anything else I can get for you?"

When they both shook their heads, she left.

"Would you like me to bless the food?" Neil asked.

"Please."

After he said grace, they added dressing to their salads.

"How do you feel about that? Selling the business, I mean."

He shoved his fork into the lettuce. "Eric doesn't want to take it over. Neither do I. Dad knows that, and has assured us he's okay with it." He began to eat.

Haley did likewise, savoring the sharp tang of the vinaigrette. She chewed slowly, her eyes glued to Neil's throat, his firm mouth and strong jaw line. A tremor shimmied up her spine. The sight of him made her feel like a sixteen-year-old again. The realization brought her to her senses. She swallowed so fast she nearly choked.

"Chief Richards said he brought Ricky Fowler in for a serious talk because a resident reported seeing him and another boy she didn't recognize bullying some of the younger boys."

Haley took a quick drink of tea and stifled a cough, surprised at the leap the conversation had taken. "Did Ricky admit it?" She eased the glass back onto the table.

"He couldn't very well deny it with an eye witness, but he won't name his pal." Neil leaned forward on his elbows.

Haley blinked, her mind racing. The study he focused on her made her heart skitter in fear—and excitement.

"Do you have anyone special in your life?"

The direct question hit her hard. She couldn't tell him that he was the only man who stirred a longing in her heart. "Not unless you count Pistol," she quipped in a forced voice, averting her eyes slightly.

He chuckled. "That's stiff competition for any guy."

The arrival of their shrimp platters provided a welcome diversion.

Chapter 8

$\mathcal{N}$eil watched Haley almost visibly shake off her thoughts. He remembered how much he had always enjoyed her sharp mind and calm quietness. He had treasured their friendship and nearly throttled Rick when he found out how the guy was deceiving her, stringing her along on the side while involved in a relationship with Darlene that he suspected was physical rather than true love.

When Rick died tragically and the truth came out, he had wanted to help Haley and not known how. His awkward attempt to reassure her hadn't lessened how hurt and used she felt. During the last few weeks until graduation, he had watched her become more quiet and controlled. In retrospect, he guessed that, if Beth hadn't already been in his life, he would have tried to date Haley.

He winked, hoping to put her at ease. "After you left town, I used to run into Leann once in a while, and I would ask about you. I understand why you left, but I'm proud of you for the way you returned when your family needed you."

Haley put down her slice of Texas toast. "Don't make me out to be more than I am."

"You're Haley West, your own self, pretty and resourceful. I'm proud to call you my friend."

She raised her palms, a flush appearing at the base of her neck. "I appreciate your assessment, but don't keep it up and force me to tape your mouth shut."

He grinned at the image. "Okay, let's go back to the issue of you not having anyone more special than Pistol. Don't you at some point in your life want a family of your own?"

She studied his face, as if judging his sincerity. "I don't think so. It took me a long time to get past letting what other people think or say dictate my life. But I did."

"Someone is always watching what we do and how we live. What's important is that we're loyal to God and challenge others to be the same."

"Sometimes I regret that I couldn't go to college, but I couldn't afford the cost or the time. I saw the military as a quick fix. It was a job, and it included housing."

"You got a hands-on education in life and survival,

and you've met every challenge life has thrown at you. That's more education than any school could ever teach you. If God has a bigger plan for you, He'll supply whatever you need, when you need it."

"You give me too much credit," she protested. "Anyhow, I've gotten used to running my own life and having my own space. I'm not sure I could trust, or be accountable to, someone else. What about you? Do you plan to marry again?"

Just like that she turned the subject to him. Neil drew a deep breath and leaned back in the chair. "I don't think so. I'm not afraid of marriage, but I wouldn't want to put another woman at risk trying to have a family."

To his surprise she reached over and placed a hand over his. The warmth of it worked its way through him. "Our lives have been different," she said softly. "But I know you've had to deal with loss as tough as mine. We both need God's help more than we need partners."

He met her look head-on. "I agree. But I still struggle with knowing what God wants of me. I'll never understand things that have happened, but I'm working toward acceptance."

"Good." She gave his hand a small squeeze and released it. Then she picked up a shrimp and dipped it in the sauce. He watched her put it in her mouth before tackling his own food.

~

Haley could avoid speaking while eating, but she couldn't stop thinking. She wanted to know more about his years after high school. She wiped her mouth, put the napkin down, and spoke more calmly than she felt.

"Time has gotten away from us. You were married and in college when I left here. Were those good years?"

He put his own napkin down. "They were hard, but good. I signed with Mizzou to play basketball, and married Beth. We rented an apartment, and she took a job in the alumni office."

He looked beyond her, as if staring into the past. "She wanted a baby more than anything, but she was willing to wait until we could afford it. At the end of four years, I finished my degree, we moved back here, and I went to work for the local police department. She worked part-time, and we began trying to have a family. "

"And you worked with your dad?" She had known most of his story, but not the details.

He nodded. "When my hours and his needs worked out together. Beth became involved in church ministries and worked a couple of days a week at the library. But she never got pregnant. Eventually we saw a doctor and were told that she would likely never be able to conceive."

"But she did."

His jaw tightened, and his eyes came back to her face. "She did. She laughed and cried and said it was a miracle. She immediately picked out a name. It would be Nick if we had a boy. Nicole, shortened to Nikki, if it was a girl."

His chin trembled for a moment, but he quickly recovered. "It was in her fourth month that the problems she had been having were diagnosed as cancer. She refused to end the pregnancy, determined to bring it to term. She didn't make it."

He stopped abruptly.

Haley reached over and pressed his hand. "I can only imagine what you went through. Beth made a very difficult decision, but she was blessed to have your love, and time with you."

"Almost seven years," he said in a near whisper. "I couldn't live in that empty house. I sold it, quit my job, and went to St. Louis. I questioned God. I raged against Him. I'm more reconciled now, but I'm still searching for what He wants of me. I don't think I could survive anything like that again."

She nodded in understanding. "The Bible says that God will never put more on us than we can bear, but some things bring us to our knees. Trials are supposed to make us stronger. I hope that's true for both of us."

He drew a ragged breath and tightened his fingers around her hand. "Are you done, or would you like dessert?"

"I'm done." She eased her hand free and reached for her purse and cap. She took some money from her wallet and placed it on the table for the waitress.

"Keep that," he ordered. "I'll take care of it."

She shook her head and put on her cap. "This was just a meal at the end of the shift, not a date or anything like that."

He snorted in exasperation. "You're so determined

to be independent and not be a mooch that you won't let others do anything for you, even buying you a meal."

Haley gave him a grim stare and sensed that he really wanted to feed her. "Okay," she relented. But she tossed another bill on the table.

He grinned. "Fair enough."

He drove back to the post office parking lot. "See you around."

Haley climbed into her Tracker and arrived home within five minutes. She took a shower and donned an old pair of comfortable shorts and a tee shirt. She had just settled in front of the television when a sharp knock sounded at the door.

She crossed the carpet to open it, and found Dillon, dressed in worn jeans and a blue plaid shirt, standing on the carport. She looked around for his pickup, but didn't see it.

He followed her gaze. "A water hose busted on the old truck. I left it at the garage and hiked here."

She pushed the screen door open. "Come on in. You should have called me."

"Nah, the walk was good for me." He stepped just inside the room and surveyed it, taking in her comfy nest at a glance. His eyes were still a bit red rimmed, but he looked and sounded better overall.

"Nice place you got here. Where's your boyfriend?"

Haley didn't bother to ask who he meant. "He's not my boyfriend. He's just a friend."

Dillon ambled to the couch and dropped onto it.

He directed a cynical gaze at her. "I remember him being a friendly kind of guy."

She flopped down beside him, and caught a whiff of fresh aftershave. Maybe that was what he had gone to Wal Mart to buy. "He is a good guy, and he's been through a lot."

"I heard you got hit by a runaway biker and took a rock to the head."

She scowled. "I can't help what you hear."

His quick update on the local gossip was surprising. No, it wasn't. Dillon had always been quick witted and informed on local happenings. He just didn't care much for academics. He was more of a hands-on kind of guy. She wondered briefly if he would resume his relationship with Kerry Alexander, his high school girlfriend. "Have you eaten?"

"Yeah. I got a burger at McDonald's. What I'd like now is a shower." He brushed back a stray lock of sandy brown hair and pushed to his feet.

Haley pointed toward the hallway. "Your room is on the left. Make yourself at home. You're welcome to stay as long as you need."

He headed that way.

"While you're in the shower, I'll run out and get some ice cream," she called after him. "We'll have Coke floats."

"You know I can't turn that down," he answered as the door slammed.

She did. She grabbed her purse and left the house. At the grocery store she purchased the ice cream and responded absently to the checker's friendly chatter as she paid the bill. On the way home, she pictured the pleasure Dillon would get from such a simple thing as a Coke float. How long had it been since he had enjoyed one?

He sat watching television when she entered the house. She held the bag out to him. "Cokes are in the fridge."

He grinned as he stood and took it. "I'll make the floats."

An hour later, Dillon took his empty glass to the kitchen and rinsed it. When he came back, he hooked a thumb toward the hallway. "I think I'll go to bed early. I haven't been sleeping too well lately, and I'm beat."

She waved him on. "Help yourself. I plan to turn in soon as well."

Tuesday morning Haley crawled into a uniform and ate a bowl of cereal at the table with Dillon. He refused to take her to work and keep her vehicle, insisting his truck would be ready that day and he would enjoy the hike to the garage to get it. Wishing she could do more to help him, but thankful that he was at least accepting a place to stay, she left for work.

At the end of her shift, Haley made quick work of her checkout tasks and headed home. To her surprise, Dillon was already there.

"My truck wasn't ready," he called from the kitchen.

Haley went to the doorway and found him stirring a pot of what smelled like spaghetti. "This is a pleasant surprise. I could get used to having a cook in residence."

He grinned over his shoulder at her. "Get changed, and you can fix some garlic bread. I have everything laid out."

She saluted. "Yes, sir."

His chuckle sounded good as she took off for her bedroom. Dillon had changed. His eyes were brighter, his expression more open. She knew he carried grief for what they had lost. He and Reba had been closer than any of them while growing up. She could only imagine what he had been through.

Haley changed into comfortable slacks and blouse and rejoined her brother in the kitchen. She took care of the garlic bread and set the table.

After they ate, Dillon took the garbage to the trash can on the carport. When he returned, they made more Coke floats and settled on the couch to watch the ballgame. When it ended, Dillon got to his feet. "I think I'll go for a walk."

When he was gone, Haley muted the television as the post-game commentator recapped the baseball game. She stretched out on the couch and dozed.

As from far away, noises penetrated her sleep-dulled brain. A loud crash, and then shouts. She bolted upright and listened.

The noises were coming from up the street. Dillon had gone out there. Heart pounding, she dashed to the door and shoved her feet into her shoes. She stepped out onto the front porch and peered up the street. Shadowy forms came from houses and ran to where a car, vaguely illuminated by a streetlight, rested against a tree. Someone knelt in the street.

Panic impelled her into motion. "Dillon?" she yelled, her voice shrill.

A cluster of people stood around a crumpled body at the edge of the street.

"Who is it?" Haley demanded, edging her way between two gawking women. As soon as she saw the shirt, she knew. She fell to her knees beside Dillon amidst pieces of glass that littered the pavement. A shattered headlight?

A pool of blood oozed from a huge gash on his arm. He didn't move. "It's my brother," she screamed, slapping at the hands that gripped her shoulders when someone tried to pull her away. She ran a hand over his chest. As she did, he groaned.

He's alive. Thank you, Lord.

Taking a deep breath, she clamped down on her emotions and fought off dizziness. "Dillon, can you hear me?"

His eyes opened a slit. "Yeah," he whispered. "What happened?"

"I don't know. Please don't try to move. I need to get my phone and call for help."

He closed his eyes.

"I'm sorry, I'm sorry," a woman's voice wailed from the other side of Dillon's body.

Haley looked up and recognized Mrs. Reed, her neighbor from four houses up the street.

"I've already called 911," the woman said unsteadily. "I was coming home from a meeting, and that boy on a bike shot out from behind a house into the street." She pointed.

Haley looked over where another group of residents hovered in a circle. A bicycle lay at the edge of the yard.

"I swerved to miss him, but your brother was faster," Mrs. Reed continued between sobs. "He jumped into the street and shoved the bicycle out of my way. But I hit him. I'm sorry, I'm sorry," she wailed repeatedly.

"The boy's okay," someone called from across the street. "That guy saved this kid's life."

"Help is on the way," another voice yelled. "They should be here any minute."

Haley held Dillon's hand and prayed.

Chapter 9

*N*eil had just noted the seven o'clock time when his cell phone rang. He left his mother's bedside and stepped into the hallway to answer it.

"There's been an accident at Haley West's residence." Chief Richards' voice was a sharp staccato bark. "We're on our way. So is an ambulance. I thought you might want a heads-up."

His gut twisted. "She was hurt?"

"Her brother was hit by a car." The phone went silent.

Neil stuck his head inside the doorway. "Dad, I have to leave." He took off in a sprint up the corridor. When he parked alongside Haley's yard, a stretcher was being loaded into an ambulance. A half block beyond that, two men supported a boy between them and put him into a police car. Neil was out of the Cherokee almost before the motor stopped running.

"Haley, wait up," he called, seeing her getting into her vehicle. He ran across the yard and caught her arm. "You don't need to be driving. I'll take you to the hospital."

She stared at him, pale faced and clearly shaken. She opened her mouth as if to object, and then closed it. He led her to his Cherokee as the ambulance took off, siren screaming. The car with the boy followed it.

"How are you?" he asked Haley as he put the Cherokee in reverse and worked it back around to follow the flashing lights.

"Okay," she whispered, her posture rigid.

"What happened?"

She faced him, as if just realizing where she was and who she was with. "After supper Dillon went out for a walk. I fell asleep. Sounds of a crash and shouts woke me. I ran up the street and found him. Mrs. Reed swerved to miss a kid on a bicycle. Dillon shoved the bike to safety, but he was hit."

"Was he conscious?"

She nodded, her hands twisted together in her lap. "He groaned and opened his eyes for a few seconds. When I asked him if he could hear me, he said yes. He asked what happened and closed his eyes. I was afraid he had died."

"He's tough. He'll make it. God has work for him to do around here." Neil glanced both ways and shot into the traffic.

"He doesn't even have a job."

"He will. But that's not what I'm talking about. I called him after lunch today and invited him to go with me to a D.A.R.E. meeting at the high school. Eric had asked me to attend and help the D.A.R.E. officer with the question and answer session at the end of it."

"Why did you invite Dillon?"

"I'm not sure. I guess I just wanted to befriend him, let him know he's welcome back."

Even if you don't live here.

"I think it worked out well. When a student posed a sarcastic question about drinking not being harmful, Dillon stood and gave the group a two minute lesson about just how harmful drinking can be to a life, citing his personal example. You would have been proud of him."

Haley's face twisted in pain, and her hand covered her trembling mouth. Tears tracked down her cheeks. "Then he came home and saved a kid's life," she choked in a strangled voice.

Neil shoved the gas pedal to the floor and passed the cars, one at a time, that were between them and the ambulance. He saw her grip the handle above the door for balance.

They followed the red and blue flashes from the light bars of the police and medical vehicles. Within minutes they followed the caravan into the hospital parking lot, and were at the emergency entrance by the time the ambulance attendants emerged from the vehicle.

They were only allowed as far as the admitting desk. Haley answered rapid questions as Dillon was wheeled inside.

"That'll do for now," the clerk said, glancing over the papers. "You may go to the waiting room."

Neil escorted Haley down the corridor and around a corner to a rectangular room furnished with functional, but unimaginative and uncomfortable, furniture. He cleared a magazine off the end of a sofa and guided her down onto it. He sat next to her.

~

Haley glanced at her watch and pulled her phone from her purse. "I need to call Leann."

"I'm coming," her sister said when Haley told her what had happened.

"Don't speed," Haley warned. She visualized her reckless sister making the hundred mile trip from Springfield to Skyview in breakneck time.

"I think you should call your boss and tell him what happened and that you won't be in to work tomorrow," Neil said when she disconnected.

Haley made the call. Then she faced Neil. "Why do bad things keep happening to Dillon?" She blinked against the tears burning the backs of her eyes.

Neil pulled her to his chest. "He saved a kid's life. Be proud of him."

A doctor entered the waiting room. His eyes went to Haley. "Are you the sister?"

Haley nodded and bounced to her feet, forgetting to breathe. *He's not dead. He's okay. That's what he's come to tell us. It has to be.*

"Your brother is fortunate," the doctor informed her in a clinical tone. "My biggest concern is the blow he took to the head when he hit the pavement. He has a dislocated and badly bruised hip and has lost quite a bit of blood, but his overall prognosis is favorable."

The tears that had been held in check burst free and streamed down her cheeks. "Thank you, doctor." *Thank you, Lord.*

Neil's arm came across her back, warmth and strength flowing from him.

Her hoarse whisper sounded strange to her own ears. "When may I see him?"

"He's asleep, but you may step into his room for five minutes. He's still in ICU, but we'll move him to a regular room tomorrow." He turned to go.

Haley didn't object to Neil's grip on her arm as the doctor led them to the ICU and left them at the door. When they stepped inside, Haley's breath caught at the sight of Dillon lying pale and quiet in the bed, hooked up to tubes and IV bags. A nurse straightened from adjusting the covers over him and turned to face them. "Only five minutes," she cautioned before leaving.

Haley approached the bed and placed a hand over one of Dillon's. She squeezed it and stood praying in silence for long moments, thanking God for sparing his life and pleading for his well-being. Neil's presence provided support and comfort. The five minutes ended all too soon, and the nurse returned. "I have to ask you to leave now, but I'll let you know when you can return in an hour."

"Do you want to go home?" Neil asked when they were back in the hallway.

Haley shook her head. "I want to wait for him to wake up. I need to hear him speak."

"I understand." He escorted her back to the waiting room and resumed the seat they had vacated earlier.

With gentle hands he gripped her shoulders and turned her face toward him. "I know you think your family's difficult circumstances determine what people think of you, but that's not true. I don't care where you were born, or what kind of problems you have. Get it through your thick head that I care about you."

He pulled her tighter, and his arms made her feel safe. As Haley nestled into his chest, a sweet lethargy seeped through her. Between them her heartbeat thumped an erratic tempo.

A soft breath escaped her, and a hand went up to stroke the strands of his dark hair. When his lips touched hers, she melted against him. When they brushed her mouth a second time, her eyes drifted shut.

"How do you end up in the middle of everything?"

The voice made Haley and Neil draw apart with a start.

Haley stifled a groan as she turned to face Darlene Fowler, whose excessive black eyeliner reminded her of a raccoon. The reporter's words had been said in an outwardly jocular manner, but Haley recognized the fakeness of it. Her stomach muscles knotted.

"I came for a story, but it seems you're otherwise

...occupied. Would you prefer that I come back later?"

Haley pulled herself together and responded in what she hoped was a polite tone. "Now is as good a time as any. How may we help you?"

Darlene perched on the edge of a chair facing them, took a pen from her purse, and balanced a notepad on her lap. "Tell me about the accident. Explain what happened. What is your brother's condition?"

Haley eased away from Neil, needing distance between them. Then she carefully repeated the story to Darlene. "Dillon is expected to survive, but he's still unconscious."

"Was he drinking?"

"He was not," Neil spoke up instantly. "He was simply out for a walk and saved a kid from serious injury or possible death."

Darlene stiffened, but maintained her poise. "Who is the boy he saved?"

"I don't know, but I plan to check on him."

"I can help with that."

The new voice made all three of them look up, and Haley found Brooke Whitney Channing standing in the doorway. Her girlhood friend came to sit next to Haley and embraced her in a warm hug. Then she pulled back and faced Darlene. "I don't know details, but I recognized Dr. Braxton downstairs, and he told me where to find Haley. He also said that they checked the boy, pronounced him fine, and sent him home. The boy's name is Mickey Osborn."

The Doctor Braxton she referred to was Kelly

Braxton, who had graduated from Skyview High School three years ahead of them.

Darlene gasped.

Haley looked up to see that the reporter's face had gone white. "What's wrong?"

Darlene shook her head and visibly gathered her composure. "Nothing. I just thought of something I should have done earlier." She glanced down at her notes. "I think I have enough here for the story. I need to go."

With that, she practically ran from the room.

"What was that all about?" Neil asked.

"If I'm not mistaken, that's her son's best friend," Haley said slowly, her thoughts spinning. Could he be the pal Ricky would not name for Chief Richards? She stored the idea in the back of her brain.

"I'll text Pastor Bill," Neil interjected, punching buttons on his phone.

Haley acknowledged his words with a nod. She would love for the pastor to visit Dillon.

Brooke took one of her hands. "I'm sorry, Haley. I understand Dillon will be all right. I was on my way home from visiting Paige at the lake when she called and told me about the accident. I turned around and came straight here. Paige said she would call Kelsey, and they'll see you as soon as they can. Tell me how it happened."

Haley's nerves relaxed a bit at Brooke's comforting presence. She, Paige, and Kelsey had always been the ones who were there for her, their friendship a mutual thing. She scooted over a bit as Brooke released her.

After she finished repeating the story, the three of them alternated between talking and staring at the clock as the minutes ticked by with excruciating slowness. At ten o'clock, Leann came rushing into the waiting room. Slight of frame at only five feet one, Haley's baby sister had a small oval face, brown eyes, and light brown hair. She hurried to Haley's side and squeezed in between her and Neil. Neil and Brooke both moved to a sofa across the room.

"I left five minutes after you called. Tell me more about what happened. How is he?" Her voice held the shrillness of panic.

"He's sleeping. The doctor said he should recover. We're waiting to see him again."

Leann stared at Haley, tears winding down her face. "Where was he when he got hurt?"

"He was spending the night at Haley's." Neil's explanation was simple, yet gentle, when Haley had trouble speaking.

Leann's eyes grew wild. "Why did he get hit?"

Haley explained once again what had happened, beginning to feel like a broken record.

Leann's hand went over her mouth, her head shaking silently back and forth.

Haley reached over and placed a hand over her sister's. "It's been nearly an hour since we last visited Dillon. We should be able to see him soon. We can only go in two at a time, so you take the next turn."

Brooke came back to Haley's side and gave her another hug. "You have your family now, so I'll run along. But I'll be in touch. And I'll call Paige and Kelsey and give them an update."

As Brooke left, Pastor Bill arrived. Kindness gleamed from his blue eyes behind silver framed glasses. Behind him, a group of people who appeared to be an upset family filed into the opposite side of the room. The place was beginning to feel like Grand Central Station.

After Haley repeated her tale for the pastor, he led them in prayer. Then the little group sat in silence until a nurse came and said Dillon was awake and they could take turns visiting him.

As promised, Leann was given the first turn.

"Will you come home with me?" Haley asked when she returned to the waiting room and the pastor took the next turn to see Dillon.'

Leann swiped at her eyes. "I have a test in the morning at nine o'clock, but I need to talk to Michelle. If I spend the night with her, we can finalize plans for her to move in with me next month."

Leann and Michelle had been best friends for years and planned to room together all through college, but Michelle had a summer job locally and would join Leann for the beginning of the regular semester.

"I hope Dillon will be staying with me when he gets out of here."

Leann gave her a weak smile. "Good. I'm glad my room is there for him. I'll leave early enough in the morning to stop by and see him again. I hope he can talk to me by then."

She gave Haley a quick hug and left.

"We had prayer," the pastor informed them when he emerged minutes later.

"You ready to go home?" Neil asked Haley after their visit to Dillon's room. "The nurse said he'll sleep all night. Tomorrow's the holiday and you don't have to work, so you can come see him whenever you want. I don't want to rush you, but I don't want you collapsing from fatigue and unable to visit when he's awake."

Haley hesitated a moment before agreeing. "You're right."

It was midnight when they pulled into her driveway. "Is it too late for you to drink coffee?"

The beam from the corner streetlight showed his grin. "I can drink coffee anytime."

As he emerged from the vehicle, Haley saw him reach down and take a small bag from the floorboard. She started to comment about it, but decided it was none of her business.

"What can I do?" he asked as she prepared the coffee.

She pointed at a section of cabinets. "Mugs are in there."

He took the bag he carried and left it on the coffee table before taking two mugs from the cabinet and placing them on the counter. They both went to the living room and settled to wait for the coffee to brew.

"You had a funeral this afternoon, didn't you?" Haley asked, feeling guilty that she had forgotten, and realizing what a long day he had endured.

He inhaled deeply. "I did. It went well. The lady

was elderly and had a small family. She lived a strong Christian life, so it was an easy funeral to conduct, if there is such a thing."

"I understand what you mean, but what about the ministry part? Did you feel stressed?"

He mused for a few moments before answering. "No, I didn't," he said at last. "In fact, I felt like God had His hand on me."

Haley's emotions were tangled. She loved spending time with Neil, even dreamed of more in spite of herself. But no way could she ever fit into the ministry.

Stop, Haley. Don't go there.

"What did you make of Darlene Fowler's manner this evening?" he asked.

"Darlene's never been friendly toward me," she said stiffly.

His look portrayed understanding. "I know. She knew Rick liked you."

"She's never said so, but I've often thought she did."

"That's not what I was asking about, though. I meant her reaction just before she left the hospital."

Haley shrugged. "I assumed she wanted to check on her son's friend."

"I think those two boys are headed for trouble."

She agreed. "Ricky's father died before he was born. He has a little brother whose dad was Darlene's first husband, and there's been another husband since then. Darlene's sour on life, and the boy seems to be imitating her attitude."

"Ricky would be ten or eleven, if I remember correctly."

She nodded. "His brother is three or four years younger. I'm not sure what kind of child care arrangements Darlene has while she works."

Neil went to get their coffee. "I'm afraid they're allowed to run free a lot, at least Ricky."

Haley tapped her memory bank. "I see them at Darlene's parents' house sometimes when I'm delivering in that part of town."

He returned with two mugs and placed them on the coffee table. After they were empty, he picked up the bag he had left there earlier and handed it to Haley.

Curious, she opened it and peeked inside. Then a slow grin spread across her face. "You're worried about my physical condition?"

"I was in a sport shop this morning and saw it. It reminded me of you."

She took the pink jump rope from the bag and inspected it. "Looks like it needs testing. Come on."

He followed her down the hallway. Inside the combination office-den, she stepped on the piece of outdoor carpeting in the center of the floor. Then she began to turn the rope, conscious of him leaning against the doorframe, watching.

Chapter 10

*N*eil watched in amazement as the rope's speed increased in Haley's hands. Alternating feet, jumping higher and faster, she was soon doing double unders—turning the rope twice under her feet. As she slowed a bit and worked the rope in a crisscross pattern, he studied her. This woman was not the insecure teenager he had known. Yet this past week the protectiveness he had always felt toward her had grown into something broader, something resembling a personal complication not in his plans. He didn't need this. The stirring in the region of his heart was foolish. Yet he *had* to be with her.

She came to a sudden stop. "It's a good rope.

Thank you."

He puffed his cheeks and blew out a whoosh of air. "You really know how to use that thing. I'm impressed. No wonder you're in great physical condition."

She shrugged and placed the folded rope across the back of the desk chair. "My job is the main reason for that. But it's a great way to work off tension. Ten minutes of jumping is the equivalent of an eight-minute mile, and it doesn't cause the knee damage that can result from running. The impact of the jumps is absorbed by the balls of the feet rather than the heels."

He could tell by her rushed speech and the slight color in her face that compliments made her uncomfortable. He grinned and shoved away from the doorframe. "I jump sometimes in workouts, but no fancy footwork like that."

"I liked jumping in P.E. classes," she said dismissively. "In the army some of us liked it so much we became competitive. Our drill sergeant encouraged us."

"Would you like me to go with you in the morning to visit Dillon?"

She tipped her head. "Are you trying to baby me?"

"If you'll let me." Yes, he wanted to take care of her, but he wanted her with him, period. "We'll visit both our mothers at the nursing home after we leave the hospital," he added as an extra persuasion.

Now she smiled. "All right."

He reached over and brushed back a stray wisp of

hair that fluttered around her temple, noting the remaining traces of tension in her mouth. It was good to see that some of her uneasiness had melted during the brief exercise session.

The touch of her skin made his breath catch and his heart race. Until this week he had not thought about kissing another woman. He still felt married to Beth. His mind knew she was gone, but his heart had never accepted the reality of it. He thought she would approve of him going on with his life, but he hadn't felt free to do that. These new feelings were confusing.

Haley's eyes locked on him, as if she felt the same jumble of emotions. He thought he saw a tremor in her hands as she edged away from him.

He placed his hands on her arms and stopped her retreat. She tilted her head to study his face, and a hand came up to his shirt collar. "What do you want?" she whispered.

The question touched him, made him want to take away everything that hurt or threatened her. His chest tightened, and the truth came out. "To finish what we started at the hospital."

Her mouth opened slightly. "That's not smart. The last thing in either of our plans is a serious relationship."

"True," he said with candor. "I didn't plan this, but I accept that there's something very powerful between us."

She tilted her head. "Animosity?"

"Nope. Maybe there was a touch in the beginning, but it's far different now." He lifted a hand to stroke her cheek, and then cupped her chin in his palm. He pulled her to him, so close he could feel her heartbeat drumming against his chest. It felt so good to have her there, meeting him halfway. When his lips pressed against hers, she leaned into him. Pure joy exploded in him as he absorbed her sweetness.

He lifted his mouth and rested his forehead against hers a moment before pulling back, watching her visibly gather her composure. The expression on her face made him wonder how much damage Rick had done. He placed his palms on the sides of her face.

"Why are you still single, Haley?"

Her body stiffened. "I can take care of myself. I don't need a husband to look after me."

"I'm afraid you've let one rotten experience ruin your feelings about men, and marriage. I know you grew up feeling insecure and inferior because you were poor and didn't participate in a lot of school activities. I also know that your family counted on you. You were gentle and sweet natured, and you still are. But you maintain distance between you and any man who shows interest in you. Except me. Why is that?"

Her teeth raked her lower lip, her eyes avoiding his. "You're my friend. You always treated me as an equal." Now her face lifted, and she met his gaze. "At least that's what I believed until I overheard your comment to that group of kids."

Her words stung. He cringed with regret. "I never said anything negative about you. I just didn't defend you the way I should have. I didn't want to start an argument. Knowing some of those girls, and how jealousy works, I knew it would just urge them on if I said anything. I'm sorry. I've always considered you my equal, or better."

"I've put the past behind me," she said quietly. "When I graduated, I couldn't get away fast enough and never planned to come back. But I did. I went after an independent life, had some good years, and then found myself needed here again. But I'm no martyr."

"Do you wish you could break free and leave again?"

He watched her consider her words before answering.

"I've accepted that I should be here, that apparently this is where I have to be. I have a responsibility to see that Mom is taken care of, and God provided a good job when I needed it. My needs are provided, and I'm thankful that I can do at least a little for her."

"As well as the needs of some others?" He gave her a lopsided grin.

She shrugged. "Sometimes."

"You still haven't answered my question. Why have you let me get so close to you?"

Her eyes focused somewhere beyond him. "I'm not sure. Why *are* you getting so close?"

He took a deep breath. The question was fair. "I guess I'm not real sure either. I've always liked you."

"And tried to protect me."

"Guilty. But that protectiveness seems to be developing into something I'm not sure I'm ready to handle."

She looked into his eyes, all the way to his soul, it seemed. "You left here for different reasons than I did, but it still involved hurt. I know you loved Beth and that the grief was too much for you. You needed change."

"Like you, I never expected to come back, but I should. Mom's not going to completely recover. I have to make a decision soon."

"But not because of guilt."

He emitted a heavy sigh. She truly did understand. "I can't move back unless I know for sure it's God's will for me. Finding you here and connecting like this has been a surprise."

"I didn't expect it either," she admitted.

He pulled her to him and held her close for a few moments. Then he placed a kiss on her forehead and released her.

He left her house, not wanting to leave her alone. Truth was, he hated to leave her at all. Kissing her was probably a mistake, but it was one he was going to be powerless to keep from repeating. The very thought made him light up inside. Could he be in love with her?

~

After Neil left, Haley showered and crawled into bed, but her mind refused to stop spinning. Scary truths stared at her, the biggest one being that she loved Neil Bronson.

She knew God loved her, but felt intimidated by Him. She used to pray that God would make her lovable, give her a husband and family, but always in the recesses of her mind had lingered the disaster with

Rick. Eventually she had accepted that she was not the type of girl guys wanted for romance. They wanted her friendship, her help with their homework, her ideas for school assignments. But when they asked a girl for a date, it was always someone from the popular crowd, someone like Darlene.

"I'm sorry, Lord. I shouldn't complain. I have a comfortable life. My health is good. I have a good job, friends, and You.

She thought back. When Rick had sought her out, she had been almost desperate for companionship, conversation, a feeling of belonging. The experience had shattered her dreams of love and trust. Now she was older and wiser, and having those things didn't seem as important.

She had learned some valuable lessons. Wanting something couldn't make it happen, and she could live life alone and be content to do it. Those were good lessons. In hindsight she could see that they were ones God had taught her so she could grow.

Now she found herself wanting to trust a man again, but she feared she wouldn't survive the pain if she dared trust Neil and he broke her heart. She had immersed herself in work and continued to help her family, pretending an outward façade of self-assurance and strength until it had become real. She had even learned to love herself enough to allow others to love her, had become dedicated to God. But now she felt threatened, vulnerable, in her safe little life.

What was love? What did it mean? In her teens she had experienced infatuation, a physical attraction based more on fantasy than reality. Now she could look back and recognize it for the shallow, self-serving experience it had been. What she felt now was love, the real thing, an unconditional emotion that centered on the needs of the other person and never ceased giving.

Just how long her feelings for Neil had been love, she was not sure. It was a startling, glorious thing she had never expected to find. If only there was a future in it.

Lord, if loving Neil is wrong, please remove it from my heart and point me toward the life you have planned for me. Help me to accept Your will, whatever it is.

She prayed herself to sleep.

The phone woke Haley the next morning. Groggy, she reached over and snatched it from the bedside table. "Yeah."

"Good morning, grumpy. Want to hit a restaurant for breakfast before we visit Dillon?"

Brought awake by Neil's voice, she crossed an arm over her eyes.

"I'll pick you up in thirty minutes," he said before she could invent an excuse.

Haley aimed a mock salute at the dead phone and muttered, "Aye, aye, boss." Then she lay there a few more moments, until the thought of breakfast made her crawl out of bed. She put on a pair of navy slacks and a white tee shirt with the school mascot across the front. She had bought it from a teenager selling them for a school fund raiser.

A peek out the window showed a day already bright with hot sunshine. She grabbed her purse and ran out to meet Neil when he pulled into her driveway.

As they entered a restaurant a few minutes later, they met Darlene Fowler on her way out. She pretended not to see them and kept going.

Neil shivered after Darlene exited. "I felt the chill as she passed. The lady has a problem."

"She never liked me and is still critical of me, but she has no quarrel with you."

"I suspect she's having trouble with her son, and because you've been connected to that problem—by getting hurt, no less—her anger and frustration have transferred to you." He led her to a table and pulled out a chair.

"And on to you because you're with me," she added as she slid onto it.

He eyed her across the table, a teasing grin on his face. "I can brave most anything to spend time with you. Do you remember what the evangelist Billy Graham used to say about his critics?"

She couldn't help but grin. "Yeah, he said he never answered them."

"He also said that if the mailman stopped every time a dog barked, he'd never get the mail delivered."

"Count on you to bring my job into it," she huffed in mock exasperation. Then she directed her attention to the menu.

After their meal, they went to the hospital to see Dillon. He had been moved to a regular room and was sleeping, but he opened his eyes when they entered.

Haley approached the bed and placed a kiss on his forehead, so glad to see him awake, if not alert, that she couldn't speak.

"Get me out of here," he said weakly.

Haley swallowed and forced back tears. "Don't be silly. You need to stay here awhile."

He closed his eyes, and then reopened them. "Can't. No insurance." His speech was thick and slow.

"Don't worry about it." She fought to keep her voice from breaking. "You took on a car to save a kid."

His brow creased in confusion. "Doesn't sound like me. It's pretty hazy."

"You have to let me take care of you."

Silence stretched as he absorbed her words, the process hindered by medication.

She gripped his hand. "As soon as the doctor will release you, I want to take you home with me. I ate the last of your spaghetti."

Distracted by the off topic remark, his expression lightened. Then his eyes beamed past her to Neil.

Neil stepped forward and touched hands in a semblance of a handshake. "Sure glad to see you're okay."

They visited a few more minutes, with no further mention of insurance or bills. Haley hoped Dillon forgot. She would set up a payment plan if necessary.

When her brother's eyes drifted closed, they left for the nursing home.

"I feel like one of those visiting nurses making calls, or a church member making visits," Haley remarked as they walked down the corridor. She followed Neil into his mother's room.

Jim Bronson sat at his wife's bedside. Haley felt self-conscious at intruding on them. She was an outsider, someone their handsome son hauled around with him because—she wasn't quite sure why. But the smile on Jim Bronson's face quickly put her at ease.

She had known the elder Bronsons growing up, but her encounters with them had been at church or their business, often during times of bereavement and stress. She knew they were committed Christians and went beyond the normal range of services to families during times of loss, providing food and drinks in the family room, and contacting their own spiritual mentors for families who had none of their own. Jim had even been known to take on that ministry role personally.

Mrs. Bronson, propped up in the bed, smiled in recognition. "Haley West. It's good to see you. Jim tells me you've been around before, but I was busy sleeping." She extended her arms in a way that made it impossible for Haley to avoid a hug. Such open affection was not natural to her reserved nature.

"How is your brother?" Lillian asked when Haley stepped back. "Jim's been telling me about all that has happened to the two of you."

"Dillon's improving and already begging to leave the hospital."

Mrs. Bronson snorted. "Men are so impatient. They'd go crazy if they had to be confined like this." She moved her in a sweeping arc that encompassed the room.

Haley relaxed in the total acceptance she sensed from this gentle couple.

"They also make big decisions when we're not around to carry our weight," the woman continued, her face losing its animation. "Jim says he wants to sell the business, and I feel responsible."

"It's time," her husband interrupted, reaching over and gripping her hand. "We're both past sixty-five and have earned the right to slow down and enjoy our golden years." He put a mocking emphasis on the word golden.

Haley wished she knew a way to help them.

They visited a few more minutes, and then went on down the hall. They found Haley's mother sleeping, so they only stayed a couple of minutes and left rather than disturb her.

Chapter 11

*N*eil dropped Haley back at her house and went to the funeral home to see how Cheryl, the secretary, was getting along on her own. He settled at his dad's desk to go through the stack of papers she had left for him.

The intercom buzzed. You have a call on line one," Cheryl's voice announced.

He answered. "Bronson."

"Can you have a sandwich with me at noon?" It was Sam Richards.

"Sure. Where?"

"Would you mind making it a burger in my car where I can monitor my radio? It's also more private," he added in a tone that Neil couldn't quite interpret.

"I have no problem with that."

"Good. I'll pick you up at eleven forty-five."

At noon they sat in the chief's cruiser at the edge of town and shared a large order of fries with their burgers.

Sam took a long swig of coffee from the mug he kept in the cruiser and had refilled at various eating places throughout the day. "We're patrolling more closely than in the past. No bikes are allowed on the streets or sidewalks after dark. I wish we had you back here for good."

The abrupt change of subject threw Neil for a moment. "I'm thinking about it. My parents could use my help."

"And you've found a special interest here." His words and tone held meaning.

Neil didn't bother to deny it. "I guess I could take over the business for Dad, but I ..." He shrugged, his voice trailing to silence.

The chief's head bobbed. "You don't really want to, but you feel duty-bound to take care of them. I get it. Will you level with me?"

Neil hesitated, afraid of what he might be committing to. "I'll try."

"What would it take to get you back here permanently?"

Neil placed his soft drink cup in the console, stalling. "I guess I'd have to be certain it's what God wants."

"What if you had more options?"

He studied his former employer and fellow church

member. "What do you mean?"

Sam faced him head-on now. "What would you think if I told you I don't plan to run for chief again?" He sounded suddenly ill at ease, tentative.

"You're retiring?"

Sam grimaced. "The doctor says I am. The question is whether I can finish this term. I'm ...uh ..." He pressed his lips together. After a moment he cleared his throat. "My old ticker's been bad for a while. It's getting worse. Doc says I have to hang it up or check out."

Neil's heart ached for his old mentor. "I'm sorry to hear that."

"I want to finish the term," Sam continued. "If I can't, the city council will have to appoint an acting chief, promote someone."

Neil knew the officers well. "I'm sure Harmon or Quick would jump at the opportunity."

Sam shook his head. "Harmon's too young and makes too many mistakes. Quick has some issues on the home front that could interfere with his work. I think it's too much for him. What I'd like to do is finish this year and support you as a candidate to replace me. But you would need to move back here and reestablish your residency before you could qualify. You could run your dad's business until it sells or you're elected."

He paused to give Neil time to assimilate his news. Then he spoke again. "There's another factor to consider."

Neil frowned, not understanding. "What factor?"

"What are you running from?"

His muscles tightened. This was turning into an interrogation. "What do you mean?"

"I mean there's another option, one I think you're dodging."

So Sam knew.

Sam nodded, reading him like a textbook. "You've been filling in for preachers. You took classes appropriate for the ministry while getting another degree. You've done police work and administrative work. When are you going to admit that God's calling you to preach?"

Neil swallowed. He knew Sam was perceptive, but not *how* perceptive.

"No answer, huh?" Sam challenged when he didn't argue.

"I'm not sure. No one has ever confronted me about it before."

"Well, I am now." Sam's mouth did a funny little movement at the corners. "I've talked to your dad. He said if I want to risk my neck by doing it, it's my neck."

Knuckles shoved up against his chin, Neil shook his head. "I know you're a deacon at the church, but even you can't produce a church for me right here."

Now Sam grinned outright. "Wanta bet?"

Had he heard right? Neil waited in silence.

"I'm not the only one hanging it up. The pastor met with the deacons last month and told us he wants to retire at the end of the year. He plans to announce it to the church at the next business meeting and appoint a committee to search for his successor. We, the deacons I mean, would like for you to submit a resume´."

Neil brushed a hand across his face. "Wow. You've got it all worked out."

Sam shook his head. "Not really. You can't do both. What do you want to do? What does God want you to do? Will you pray about it and let me know your decision as soon as possible?"

"I can promise to do that much."

The chief's eyes suddenly grew shiny and moist. He looked the other way and made a surreptitious swipe at the corner of his eye. Then he turned back and glanced at his watch. "Gotta go to work. But there is one more thing to pray about," he added as he started the engine. "That last option would work better if you had a good woman by your side."

~

After Sam dropped him back at the funeral home, Neil met with two Chamber of Commerce members and helped them transport a pontoon and the fireworks that would be set off at that night's display from a spot out by the lake. When they asked who would stay and guard the stuff, he volunteered to stay until five.

When the other guys were gone, Neil parked his Cherokee closer to the spot and sat staring blindly over the wheel. His eyes dropped to the ring on his finger, and his mind traveled back through time. He remembered Beth's radiant glow at their wedding. But her face wasn't as clear as it used to be. He had thought she would be the only woman he would ever love and marry. Suddenly the grief that had been his constant companion for the past four years no longer stabbed so painfully. Coming home and getting involved had been a form of therapy for him.

He pressed his fingertips to his temples and ground his teeth as the finality of his loss slowly but completely sank in, rocking him with fresh pain. Beth's funeral had been the hardest experience of his life. He couldn't understand why it had happened. The sunshine had disappeared from his existence, and he had lived in a state of denial and grief, then eventually sold his home, quit his job, and left.

He opened his eyes and looked up at the heavens. "I loved her, Lord, and I know she's with You." As he sat there, hardly thinking or moving, just letting his heart beat and his mind rest, a sense of peace gradually stole over him. Then, ever so slowly, Beth's face came into focus, her lips moving in the image in his mind. She smiled, and it seemed as if she said that everything was okay. He had made her happy, and now he should go on with his life. The words "be happy" rang in his head. Then her image faded.

In its place appeared a picture of Haley. Where Beth had been full figured, warm, funny, and open, Haley was petite, cool, serious, and reserved. But she was every bit as strong and capable. Beth had possessed a self-confidence developed from growing up in a warm, supportive family, while Haley was more vulnerable and accustomed to supporting her family. Sparkling eyes and a soft mouth were attributes of both.

A more recent memory surfaced. Haley's mouth had been soft and responsive when he kissed her. Was she falling in love with him, the way he was with her? The idea no longer held such terror for him, nor did it make him feel as if he were betraying Beth. His faith had been tested, but was now stronger. He had come to rely more on God for strength.

Once again his eyes zeroed in on the ring on his left hand. He reached over and rubbed it with his right hand. Then, ever so slowly, he worked it over his knuckle and off his finger. He put it in his pocket.

When his relief arrived at five o'clock, he started the engine and drove to Haley's house. He knocked on the door.

~

Haley's traitorous heart did several extra beats when she opened the door and saw Neil, wearing khakis and a black polo shirt, standing there. She motioned him inside. "Have a seat while I change into something a little more appropriate."

"Any improvement might rattle me," he called after her as she hightailed it down the hall.

Inside her bedroom, Haley pressed a palm over her racing heart. Handsome and charming, he was of the species that couldn't be trusted. Why in the world did she keep agreeing to spend so much time with him? She knew better.

I'm lonely.

The admission tore through her. She took a steadying breath. It was an ongoing battle. She wanted to be with him. Her common sense told her to run, but the illogical part of her hungered to see more of him.

"There are sodas in the fridge," she called toward the door as she pulled a pair of tan slacks and an aqua blouse from the closet.

"I'll have something later," came his response.

Haley did a quick change, scolding herself for being nervous. Back in the living room, she leaned down to pluck her purse from the coffee table in front of Neil, and her heart threatened to explode at the sight of the bare third finger of his left hand.

He followed the path of her gaze. "It was time," he said, tugging her down beside him. "I loved Beth, and I'll never forget her. But God has given me the freedom to look to the future."

Haley swallowed, her throat gone dry. The import of his action and words had her heart pounding in her throat. Hearing him speak of the future filled her with hope—and despair. He couldn't be referring to a future for them together. No matter what he might say, he knew how unsuitable a match they would be.

"I'm happy for you," she said, trying to keep it all about him. "I can only imagine what you've been through."

He took her hands in his, stroking them with his thumbs. "You've been through a lot, too. You lost your sister and, to a great extent, your mother. Your little sister is doing well, and you seem to be reconnecting with your brother. You've never failed to help your family when they needed you." His voice had grown husky, his eyes serious and compelling.

She stiffened, uncomfortable at the flattering words. "I only did what had to be done."

He held onto her hands when she tried to pull away. "I don't know what's ahead for us, but I'm ready to consider the full range of possibilities."

She dragged in a long breath against the quickening of her heartbeat. Drowning in hope, confusion, and excitement, she swallowed hard. "That's a brave statement for a guy who doesn't know where he'll be living this time next month."

His expression clouded. "You're right. I have some important decisions to make."

This time when she tugged her hands away, he released them.

When they drove up to the church a few minutes later, Haley suffered an attack of self-consciousness as people in the parking lot waved at them. The wideness of their grins made it evident that they were taking special note of the fact that she and Neil were together.

Neil had indicated that he was ready to explore the possibilities of a relationship—apparently with her in mind. The very idea excited—and frightened—her. The knot in her stomach expanded as she stepped out of the Cherokee and walked beside him into the church. She swallowed in relief when he chose a pew near the back.

Haley felt conspicuous seated beside Neil, as if all eyes were on them, even if they weren't. She struggled to focus on the Bible lesson—until something Pastor Bill said brought her to attention.

"Love and fear go together."

Haley darted her eyes around the room. Had someone been talking to him about her? About how she feared God? How she feared love?

"We should both love and fear the Lord," he continued. "Some authority figures are loved but not feared by their subordinates, so their authority is not respected and their guidelines are not followed. Others are both feared and loved by those who serve under them, and their behavior reflects it. It's not a matter of being intimidated by God, but walking in His ways and keeping His commandments because of the deep respect we have for His person and authority."

I fear God. But I also respect Him. Haley breathed deeply as understanding seeped through her. Her respect for God mingled with her love. Warmth enveloped her as the pastor continued.

At the end of the shorter than usual Bible study, Pastor Bill closed his Bible and scanned the gathering for a moment. His expression turned somber. "Our regular business meeting isn't until next week, but there's something important the church body needs to know about before then."

All eyes became glued on him as he explained about the survey and planned sale of the school property.

"That's awful," someone wailed.

"No, it's not awful," the pastor said in a calm voice. "It's a mistake, and we have to deal with it."

"But how?" another moaned.

His gaze locked on Neil. "Will you tell them what

you've done so far?"

Neil stood and calmly related what he had researched. "The pastor has requested that we be on the agenda at next week's school board meeting," he concluded.

"What can we do before then to prepare?" the first commenter asked.

"The church can approve an amount of money for the purchase of the strip of land we need—and designate someone to attend the meeting and make an offer."

Haley couldn't help but admire the poise with which Neil handled the discussion, the way he was able to communicate the issue and at the same time soothe the anxieties of the people.

The pastor, who had been sitting quietly on a pew, returned to the podium. "Since Neil has already gotten a grip on this matter, I recommend that we name him as our representative and designate five thousand dollars for the purchase of the land. That's more than the property is worth, but it'll allow some margin in case it's needed."

"I'll make a motion to that effect," someone said.

Haley read relief on faces. They were happy to have someone handle it for them.

"I'll second it," another said.

A vote was taken, and it passed.

On their way out of the church, Kelsey caught up with them. "It's so nice to see you two here again. Neil, thank you for stepping in and helping like this. I'm looking forward to working with you in Teen College next week."

Their little group edged to one side as people filed past them. Haley's eyes went to Neil. He didn't seem bothered by her friend's acceptance of them as a couple.

"Are you two headed to the lake?" Kelsey asked.

"Yes, and we need to get going," Neil said. "I'm supposed to help set off the fireworks."

"I'll sit with Haley then," Kelsey said as she headed for her vehicle.

As the final fireworks exploded into glittering cascades of color overhead a couple of hours later, Haley and Kelsey folded their collapsible chairs as others were doing. The congested parking area started a slow exodus as vehicles wove around the grounds seeking a way out in the general disorder.

Haley gazed across the dark grounds at the shadow of the pontoon coming toward shore. When it landed, three figures stepped from it. One of them broke away and started toward them.

"Here comes your heartthrob," Kelsey said into Haley's ear.

Haley was glad for the dark that hid the blush she could feel creeping up her neck. "He's just a friend."

"Okay, if that's your story. But I have eyes and good instincts. Hi, Neil," she greeted him without a break in her speech. "I've been designated to tell Haley something, but I waited for you to join us so you can both hear it. Some folks from the church have started a fund at the bank for Dillon. They plan to raise more money to add to it."

Neil's grin could be seen in the glow of the moonlight.

"Now, don't get your back up, Haley," Kelsey pleaded when Haley's mouth dropped open in stunned surprise. "There are good people around here, and they understand how things are. They want to help, just like they do for anyone who runs into an unexpected sickness or injury that's more than they can handle. They also feel extra compassion since your brother was hurt the way he was. Don't let your pride rob them of their blessing."

"She's right, Haley." Neil's arm came across her back. "They want to help. Let them."

Haley was speechless. She feared that this was an act of pity. She should refuse it. She would if it were for herself. But she couldn't for Dillon. She closed her mouth.

Kelsey gave her a hug. "Convince Dillon to accept it and pay his hospital bill with it." She walked away.

Neil placed a finger under Haley's chin and forced her to look up at him through the darkness. "How about we stop at the Chinese restaurant for takeout? Could you come up with some coffee or tea at your place?"

She hesitated.

"Hey, aren't you hungry," he coaxed. "I am."

"How about some homemade ice cream with it?"

"You bet. Let's go."

Chapter 12

"*M*m, this is good." Seated in the rocker in Haley's living room, Neil smacked his lips and spooned another bite of the orange flavored ice cream. "What secret ingredient did you use?"

Haley laughed. "It's so simple, even you could make it. Just put two cans of condensed milk and eight cups of orange soda in the ice cream freezer, stir it good, and let it freeze while you eat your takeout." Like they had just done.

He gave her a gape jawed look of amazement. "That's it?"

Her head bobbed. "Yep. Use any flavor of soda you like."

He took another bite. "I like'em all."

Haley leaned back in the corner of the sofa and watched him. It felt so good to see him relaxed in her home, enjoying such a small thing. "You remind me of those boys I saw having such a good time yesterday."

He looked up. "How's that?"

"Happy. They had put their dog in a basket, attached it to their mother's back yard clothesline, and were zip lining it back and forth along the line, having a blast."

He laughed. "Sounds like something little boys would dream up to do." He scooped the last of the ice cream from his bowl, ate it, and took the bowl to the kitchen sink. When he returned, he sat beside Haley and pulled her to his side. "You make me happy, Haley."

She rested against him. "You make me happy, too," she admitted.

He nestled her cheek against his shoulder. "I never thought I would be drawn to another woman after Beth died. Then I saw you again. I've always liked you, but this time the attraction was a first sight kind of thing. I thought—wanted to believe—that you felt it too."

"I did," she whispered, curving an arm across his waist.

He kissed the top of her head and tightened his hold on her. "I feel happy every time I see you. There's a sense of rightness, of joy and peace, that comes from being with you."

Haley leaned back so she could look into his face,

her heartbeat quickening. "It's the same for me."

He sat up straighter and cupped her cheek in his hand. His deep-set, dark eyes pierced her. "I have to be fully honest with you. I'm having dreams of a future with you, but I have some fears—and a tough decision to make."

Her heart went still. "What do you fear?"

He drew a long breath and hesitated, as if steeling himself. "The thought of getting married and my wife getting pregnant terrifies me."

Her heart constricted. She understood. But she wanted children—his children. How could she express her feelings? "I'm not ..."

"There's more," he interrupted, a muscle twitching in his jaw.

Haley eased back, the note of tension in his voice making her heart hammer with uncertainty. He placed his hands on her forearms and held her where she had to look him in the eye. She fisted her hands to keep from reaching out to caress away the lines around his mouth.

"First, I have to decide whether to go back to St. Louis to stay, or to move back here permanently. Second, if I move back here, I have to decide whether to buy the business from my parents and run it, to run for Chief of Police, or to ...quit running from the ministry."

Haley's throat caught in a spasm, cutting off breath and speech. Had he spoken of a possible future with her, and the ministry, in the same breath?

"You're considering the ministry?" The question

came out low and squeaky.

He placed a hand on her shoulder. "Hear me out. Please?"

She stared at his earnest expression and huddled back in the corner of the sofa. She didn't verbalize permission, but he took her silence as a go-ahead.

"Chief Richards says he doesn't plan to run for reelection, and he'll support me if I want to run for the position. He also says that Pastor Bill is going to announce at the next business meeting that he plans to retire at the end of the year. The deacons want me to submit a resume´."

"To become pastor of the church?" Her brain couldn't catch up with what she was hearing.

"That's right."

"But why you? It's not a business position. It's a calling from God."

"Exactly." He rubbed at his eyes. "Sam accused me of running from that call, and he pointed out some very strong evidence. I have to spend some serious time in prayer about it. I wanted to be up front with you."

She couldn't grasp it. "I could never be a pastor's wife. Especially not here."

His serious expression morphed into one of puzzlement. "You say that as if you think there's something inferior about you, and I know that's not true."

She brushed his hands away. "Neil, I'm just a girl who grew up poor and never fit into the inner circle like you did."

He shrugged. "So? Everyone knew how smart you were, how loyal you were to your family. You even served your country. You have nothing to feel bad about. What's important is how you feel about yourself."

"Ministers need wives who will be respected by their congregations, women who are better educated than me, and who have social skills and poise."

He tipped his head. "Let's see, Jesus chose poor fishermen, a tax collector, a tent maker, and others of low birth to do His work. He was born a Jew, a people looked down upon by others."

"But he wasn't accepted in his own town," Haley pointed out. "You must be familiar with the scripture that says a prophet is not without honor, except in his own country and home. I was born and raised here. I would never be accepted as a pastor's wife in my hometown."

A sigh rose from deep within him. "Haley, your difficult experiences are what shaped you and made you strong. As for being respected in your own town, have you been mistreated here? Or ostracized?"

Her mind spun, searching for examples. "No," she said slowly as she failed to think of anyone. Then she did. "Darlene doesn't like me."

"She's bitter and unhappy, but it's not your fault. She needs our prayers."

~

Neil recognized that he had shocked Haley. He hadn't realized how strongly she would react to his revelation about the ministry. He watched her throat move in a nervous swallow.

You've had years to think about it. It's totally new to her. Is she only shocked about the ministry part? What about the part involving your future?

"How much do you believe in prayer?"

She hesitated, seeming to search for words. "I believe God answers prayer for other people, but I have trouble getting answers to my own."

How could he encourage her? "The scripture says that if two or more agree on something and ask, He'll grant it. Let's join in prayer that God will direct us, and trust that He will show us His plans for us. Will you pray with me?"

She produced a semblance of a nod and bowed her head.

He reached over and clasped her hands in his. Then he bowed his head. "Father, I ask that you would give us both clear hearts and minds. Speak to us. Make it clear what your plan is for our lives. And please work in Darlene's life. Help her find the peace and joy that only You can provide. Amen."

He stood and drew her up with him. Then he tipped her face toward his. "I hope I haven't upset you. That was certainly not my intent. All I ask is that you give some serious thought to all this and pray about it with me, keeping in mind that if we do whatever God has in mind for us, He'll equip us for it. Okay?"

Haley stared up at him. Then she wrapped her arms around his waist. "Okay."

He placed a light kiss on her forehead, released her, and went to the door. "I'll call you."

As he drove away, he pictured her standing there, looking like a little girl lost. She needed time to process and gather her self-confidence before he pressed further. He would give her that time. He had no choice.

In the meantime, he had some serious thinking and praying of his own to do. He knew that Haley possessed the strength for whatever God sent her way. If she made a commitment, she would give it her whole heart. It was himself he questioned at this point.

He gripped the steering wheel tighter. "Lord, please give me a sign, or a nudge, something that will affirm whether this tug I've felt for so long is truly your call to the ministry. Leave me with no doubts one way or the other."

~

Thursday morning Haley rolled out of bed and went to work. By nine o'clock she had her mail sorted and bundled, and hit the streets.

She did her downtown loop and moved on. Up the hill from the railroad tracks she met Pistol at his usual post and gave him a friendly scratch behind the ears. "Come on, boy. Let's get it done."

The dog trotted at her side, a silent chaperon. Haley spotted Dennis sitting on the bottom porch step at his house.

"Hi, Dennis," she greeted as she mounted the steps past him. She stuck the mail in the box and went back down to where the boy had wrapped his arms around Pistol's neck. She hated to use the boy as an innocent snitch, but she had to find a way to prevent any more accidents.

When she sat beside the dejected figure, the dog went to the sidewalk to wait. "Looks like you could use a hug."

The boy turned awkwardly and put his arms around her, his face against her shoulder. "Thank you, Miz Haley."

Haley released him and gazed down into his little round face. "What's the matter, Dennis? You look sad."

His face wrinkled. "I sad."

"Are you lonely? Where's Tommy?"

He dropped his eyes and clamped his mouth shut.

"Did he go with his friends and leave you behind?"

Dennis looked back up, his eyes blinking rapidly. "They say Dennis can't keep up."

"Well, you are younger," she pointed out.

His gaze darted up the street. "Yeah," he agreed. "I'm eight."

"And they're ten, right?" Only two years older physically, but enough to resent having a handicapped little brother tagging along and needing assistance.

"Do you know Mickey Osborn?" she asked casually.

"He's Ricky's friend. Ricky and Mickey. Ricky and Mickey," he chanted.

Haley wanted to laugh, but she didn't. She had confirmed that the two boys were friends. "I saw some boys over there playing with a dog. Are those Tommy's friends?" With a head movement she indicated the yard she meant.

Dennis nodded. "Yeah. Yeah. They Tommy's friends."

"They ride their bikes together, don't they?"

He nodded again, his head moving forward and backward with his shoulders, practically his whole body. "They ride all the time."

Haley looked up the street, and then down it. "I don't see them riding today. Why are they playing in the yard instead of riding their bikes?"

Dennis looked around, as if afraid of being overheard. "They can't."

"Why can't they?"

His mouth worked in a chewing motion, ut he didn't answer.

"Do the older boys bother them?"

His whole face twisted, and his breathing quickened. Anger radiated from him. "Mickey hit Billy with a stick."

"What? Why did he hit Billy with a stick?"

Dennis fidgeted with the buttons on his shirt. "Mickey mean to Billy. Is God mad at Mickey?"

How should she answer? "God wants us to treat one another with kindness."

Dennis bobbed his head. "I know. But Mickey's mean."

"Does he throw rocks?"

More nodding. "Tommy say Mickey hit Miz Haley with a rock."

This didn't make a lot of sense. "Why did he throw a rock at me, Dennis?"

The direction of his head movements changed. "He didn't."

"He didn't?"

"He throw at Tommy."

Mickey hit Billy with a stick and threw a rock at Tommy. This young man had probably been up to no good when he rode his bike in front of that car. So he was responsible for her brother's injuries, too. The thought made Haley angry. Mickey was headed for trouble.

"Do you know the block where that rock hit me?"

Dennis shuddered, but said nothing.

"I saw some boys at a house up there. Do you know the one I mean?"

His eyes squeezed shut. "Monsters live there. They eat me if I tell you."

"Tell me what?"

He shook his head forcefully. "Can't tell you."

"Well, can you tell me about Billy? Where is he?"

"The monsters got him." With that, Dennis visibly clamped his mouth shut, even pinched his lips together with his chubby hands.

"Dennis?" The babysitter stepped through the front door. "Oh, it's you," she said when she recognized Haley. An older woman with gray hair, she smiled in relief. "I heard voices and wondered who was talking to Dennis."

"We were just chatting." Haley stood and put her bag back on her shoulder. "See you, Mrs. Cleary."

She had taken her break a little early today, Haley decided as she headed up the street. After work she stopped by the police station and told Chief Richards about her chat with Dennis.

He rubbed his eyes. "The parents of those little

bullies will shrug it off as boyish pranks, and there's not much I can do about it legally. But I'm going to do my best to make them see that bigger trouble is ahead if they don't deal with their kids. Thanks for stopping by."

Haley visited Dillon and her mother before going home. When she arrived there, she took a cold soda from the refrigerator and settled on the sofa to read her own mail. Then she fixed herself a light meal and spent some time preparing for the beginning of Teen College Monday.

That night she lay awake a long time, going over everything that had happened that week. As she grew more relaxed, a face floated into her mind—and stayed. Darlene's unhappy frown ate at her. Their poor relationship had always hovered in the background, but coming back to live in the same small town had brought it front and center.

"What can I do, Lord? She hates me."

Love her. Pray for her. Talk to her.

"Talk to her? Lord, I can't handle confrontations. They destroy me."

I'll help you.

No matter what arguments she gave, the matter would not go away. It was late when she finally fell asleep.

During the early morning hours, Haley woke to the sound of rain pounding on the roof. It continued through the day. By the time she finished her route, she was exhausted from walking against the buffeting wind and trying to keep the mail dry under her rain gear. Thoughts of Neil had dogged her the whole time as well. He hadn't called the night before, and she couldn't help but feel neglected, even though the sensible side of her knew they both needed some space. She forced him to the back of her mind. But she could not get Darlene's image to go back there. All day she wrestled with what to do.

"Lord, I can't go see her," she said under her breath. "Darlene is tough. She'll scorn me, maybe eat me alive."

Talk to her.

By the end of her next work day, Haley knew she had run out of arguments. "All right, Lord, if she tears me to shreds, you'll have to take care of my family for me."

I already do that.

"All right, all right," she muttered while scooting out of the truck at the post office. After she finished her duties and clocked out, she hiked around the building to the newspaper office.

Pausing at the door, Haley took a deep fortifying breath before pushing it open. Inside, two women occupied desks behind the counter. Darlene's head was partially visible through the window of the office behind them. The red haired receptionist rose and came to meet her.

"I need to speak to Darlene."

"I'll see if she's busy."

Rather than wait, Haley rounded the end of the counter and followed her to the door. She peered inside the room where Darlene sat at her desk.

"Do you have time to see Haley West?" the receptionist asked.

Darlene looked up from her computer screen. She scowled when she recognized Haley, but quickly regained her professional face. "May I help you?"

The receptionist returned to her desk, and Haley stepped inside Darlene's office. She closed the door behind her and dropped into a chair in front of the desk so she could be at eye level with her long time antagonist.

Darlene's impeccably made up face turned unfriendly. She gave her long frosted hair a flip and bristled with hostility. "Are you here to complain about Ricky?"

"No, I come in peace." Haley tried to inject lightness into her voice, but it came out weak.

Darlene leaned back in her chair, her gaze speculative. Her nails tapped on the desk. "That leaves news or something personal. Which is it?"

Haley stiffened her spine. Then, in a burst of unexpected courage, she decided to shoot from the hip and looked Darlene in the eye. "I know you don't like me. I don't expect to convince you to change your mind, but I would like to clear the air a little bit. I know you've been cold to me over the years because you think I had an intimate relationship with Rick Montgomery behind your back," she rushed on before she could chicken out. "I want to settle that question for you. Yes, he was friendly with me, and we spent some time together. But, in spite of the pressure he put on me, we were never intimate. That's not to say we wouldn't have been if things had continued," she said candidly. "But we'll never know. He had dated several girls, and I knew you were one of them, but I was too naïve to realize how close the two of you actually were. So I certainly didn't slip around behind your back."

Darlene sat speechless, apparently struggling to take in the rushed recitation. Then she leaned forward, palms spread open on the desk, her face flushed. "So now you're Miss Goodie Goodie. What do you expect me to do, jump up and grab you for a giant hug and a pat on the back?"

For a second Haley thought she saw a tremble in Darlene's chin, but it was so fleeting she couldn't be sure. She gulped and fought to keep her face impassive.

Darlene glanced at her watch and bounced to her feet. "I have an appointment. I'm sure you understand."

Haley beat her to the door.

"Well, Lord, I tried," she muttered as she hiked back to the parking lot. Even though she had no energy left, she drove to the hospital to see Dillon.

Chapter 13

"Can you spring me from this joint Sunday afternoon?" Dillon asked as soon as Haley entered the room where he sat propped up in the hospital bed. "The doctor says he'll release me then."

The news brought a smile to her weary face. "If you'll let me take you home with me."

"If that's what you want." His voice had turned gruff.

Haley braced herself for her next words. "Dillon, I know you're worried about the bill."

He raked a hand through his already rumpled hair. "You got that right. I may have to sneak out of here to get away without giving them a check."

"That won't be necessary."

"You're not paying it," he snapped before she could finish her explanation.

"No, I'm not," she said softly, watching his expression, and expecting him to explode when she finished. "Some people have started a fund at the bank to help you pay it."

His jaw dropped. He tried to speak and couldn't. He stared at her for what seemed like forever. But he didn't explode. Instead, his eyes grew shiny, and he shook his head. "Those people love you, Haley. They're doing it for you."

Haley sank to the side of the bed and put her arms around him. After an embrace, she eased back to look him in the eye. "I think you're right about them loving me. I'm beginning to learn that. But they're not doing this for me. They're doing it for you. They know you were hurt protecting a child, and they know you don't have a job yet. They want to help you."

He looked up at the ceiling, struggling for composure. "Tell them thank you."

They visited a few minutes, and then Haley looked at her watch. "I still need to stop at the nursing home and see Mom."

He waved her off. "Run on. But don't forget to come get me Sunday."

"I'll be here at one-thirty."

~

Neil's heart was heavy as he drove across town Saturday morning. He couldn't escape the burdens that weighed on him. For years he had felt the tug of

God's call to the ministry, but he had always made excuses and found ways to dismiss it. He had worked at jobs that served people, and had filled in for absent pastors when asked. But he had never been directly confronted about his escapism—until now.

Running for the Chief of Police position was an option, but it didn't frighten him—or excite him—the way the ministry option did.

Then there was Haley. He had tried to be honest with her—and managed to frighten her. He had spent the past two nights in prayer and resisted the urge to call her. He couldn't rush her.

Right now he had to get the yard mowed and trimmed for his dad, but the weed eater had bitten the dust. There was an old one in the shed behind the funeral home. He decided to use that one this morning and buy a new one next week. At the corner lot he turned off Main Street, drove around to the back of the building, and parked next to the storage shed. As he neared the door, an odd noise startled him. He paused and listened. It came again—a thump. Then another.

Curious, and a bit alarmed, Neil turned the doorknob. To his surprise, it opened. To his further surprise, an animal came charging toward him. He slammed the door shut just before the goat could crash into him. What in the world was a goat doing in the storage shed? And why wasn't the door locked?

He looked more closely and saw that the lock had been damaged. To convince himself he had really seen a goat, he cupped a hand over his eyes and peered through the small window beside the door. Dark eyes glared at him. It was a goat, all right, but smaller than his first fleeting impression. A rope dangled from its neck. Someone's pet?

Shaking his head, he stepped back and pulled out his cell phone, his first impulse being to call Haley. "Do you have any idea how a goat could have gotten in the storage shed at the funeral home?" he asked as soon as she answered.

There was a long silence before she spoke. "I remember seeing a group of boys with a goat several days ago. They were over in the west side of town where …"

"Where what?" he demanded when her voice trailed to a halt.

"I was thinking about who lives over there," she said evasively. "I need to see if your goat looks like the one I saw. I'll be there in five minutes." The phone went silent.

While waiting for Haley to arrive, Neil peered through the window and watched the animal wander around the room, pausing here and there to nudge at something. Suddenly it spun and charged at the door, hitting it with a thump.

Haley drove up and parked her Tracker beside his Cherokee. She hopped out, a smug grin smeared across her face. Other than that, she looked natural, yet comfortable and lovely, in simple jeans and a white blouse.

"Got your goat, huh?"

He rolled his eyes at the silly pun. "I've got

someone's goat. You tell me whose." He pointed at the window.

She edged up against the building and peeked inside. "It's the same size and color."

"So you know who owns it?"

She turned to face him, all playfulness now gone from her expression. "On the way over here I tried to picture that group of boys in my mind. I don't remember all of them, but Tommy and Dennis Bailey were there. Do you feel like taking a walk?"

He shrugged. "What do you have in mind?"

"I thought we might take your little friend up into that neighborhood and see if anyone claims him." Rather than wait for him to agree, she eased the shed door open.

Neil followed her inside and closed the door behind them. He watched as Haley quietly approached the animal and grasped the dangling rope. She tightened it and placed a hand on the young goat's head. "Good boy," she crooned. "Let's go for a walk, okay?"

His heart rate picked up at the sight of her leading a goat out of the shed and up the street.

Not far past the railroad tracks, he recognized Dennis in a yard, kicking a large rubber ball. He missed it and landed flat on his backside. Then he looked up and spotted them—and a look of wonder spread across his face. He worked himself awkwardly to his feet and came running toward them, his arms spread wide. "Billy!"

He dropped to his knees next to the goat and

hugged him like a long lost friend.

Beside Neil, Haley stared at the child—and the animal. "The kid," she whispered, barely audible. "Could it be?"

"Be what?" he whispered back.

She turned to face him. "I'm not quite sure, but I think I've made a connection. I need to talk to Dennis."

She squatted next to the boy, whose face was still buried in the goat's neck. "Is this the Billy that Mickey hit with a stick?" she asked gently.

Dennis nodded and hugged the goat tighter as it tried to break free. "Mickey teased Billy. Billy got mad and ran after Mickey. Mickey got away, and Billy ran into the sign."

"Who owns Billy?"

Dennis turned his face to one side, but maintained his hold on his ovine friend. "He lives with Cody, but we all love him."

"You mean your friends?"

His face formed a scowl. "Tommy's friends. Sometimes they let me play with them."

"Do they have some sort of club?"

His eyes widened. "You know about that?"

"I don't know what they call it."

Neil thought she had handled that nicely. She didn't say she knew they had a club, yet she managed to get information.

"They're the Biker Boys," Dennis said, nearly bursting with pride. "They ride real good."

"And is Billy the club's mascot?"

Dennis frowned and tipped his head. "Mascot?

Yeah, yeah. That's what they call him. But he's Billy."

"Billy the Kid?" she asked.

A flesh and blood smiley face beamed at them. "Yeah, he's Billy the Kid."

Neil began to understand as Haley elicited more information from Dennis.

"Did Mickey and Ricky take Billy?"

Dennis took several moments to respond. "Uh huh."

"Why didn't you tell someone?"

Dennis shook his head. "They say the monsters eat me if I tell."

"Where are the monsters?"

The boy's eyes rolled, and he gnawed on his tongue. "In that house." He shuddered.

Haley placed an arm across his shoulders. "Dennis, there are no monsters in that house. It belongs to the church beside it, and the people store their Christmas stuff in there. What you saw are the wise men and shepherd figures that stand in the manger scene during the Christmas season. One day next week you can walk up there with me, and I'll show you. Are you brave enough to do that?"

Dennis swallowed and took his time deciding. "You be with me?"

"Yes, I would."

"I think so," he finally said.

"No monsters will eat you. I promise. I need to see that Billy gets back to Cody. Okay?"

"Okay." With slow reluctance Dennis released the goat. "Bye, Billy."

"So no human kid has been kidnapped," Neil said as they walked back down the hill, Haley still leading the goat.

Haley snickered. "I believe Billy here was the abduction victim." Then her tone became serious. "From the conversation I overheard, I believe Ricky and Mickey took him and then told the boys they would kill the kid if they told anyone what they were doing."

"Why did they take him in the first place? And how did he end up in our shed?"

She drew a deep breath. "I don't know why they took him, other than to upset the boys. Bullies just want to torment their victims. As for how Billy ended up in your shed, I have no idea."

"What now?"

She turned to face him, a gleam of mischief shooting from her eyes. "Don't you think Billy would like to stroll into the police station?"

~

Sunday afternoon Haley picked Dillon up and took him home with her. She thanked God that he seemed content to stay at her house.

Monday morning when she arrived at Dennis's house, she invited him and his babysitter to accompany her up the street and showed Dennis that the vacant parsonage had no monsters in it. It took some convincing, but it was a much relieved Dennis that his babysitter took home.

The abnormally hot summer was taking a toll on the neighborhood plant growth as well as the residents. Haley consumed all the water from the big thermos she carried in the truck daily, and also accepted cold bottles of water from residents who met her at their doorways with them.

That evening's first classes at Teen College went well. They had good attendance, and the teens showed enthusiasm for the classes and projects Haley and Neil introduced. Afterward, they had ice cream sundaes and sodas with some of the teens at the local McDonald's.

About ten o'clock Haley gathered debris from their table onto a tray. "I need to go. Morning will be here before I'm ready for it."

Neil accompanied her out of the restaurant and opened the door of her Tracker for her. "Thanks for what you did tonight. The kids really liked your lesson and seem excited about tomorrow night's guest beauty expert."

Fascinated by the dimples that softened his features, Haley responded matter-of-factly. "I'm glad you think it went well."

He leaned nearer and brushed his lips across her forehead. "Dad says he'll come and monitor the last twenty minutes of tomorrow night's class so I can leave in time to attend the school board meeting. Can you get someone to do the same for you so you can go with me?"

She debated. "Kelsey will be doing the makeup demonstration, but Paige wouldn't mind coming out and monitoring the last part of the class. It'll be an excuse for a visit."

"Good. We'll go together then."

"Have you heard from Sam?" she asked before he could get away.

He paused. "No, but I'm sure he gave some parents a tough talk today."

She grinned. "He said he'll deal with it, and I'm sure he will. I'm still laughing to myself over the looks on the deputy's and Sam's faces when we walked into the station with Billy Saturday."

"They stared at the poor kid," he emphasized the word, "the whole time we were telling them what we had learned."

They were both still grinning as they parted.

~

Tuesday evening they entered the meeting room of the school district's administrative office and found seats next to the pastor. As the six board members entered and took their places at the table facing them, Neil glanced at Haley beside him. She looked cool in white slacks and a melon colored blouse.

She leaned forward to put her sunglasses in her purse and brushed against him. That was distraction enough, but the smell of her freshly shampooed hair jolted his system. More and more he wanted to share his thoughts and ideas with her, to be with her, to make life easier for her. He wanted to kiss her.

Hold up right there. You're here on business.

The first topic of discussion was the resignation of a support staff person and the need to find a replacement before the start of school. A maintenance matter followed that.

The moderator glanced at his notes. "Next on the

agenda is South Side Bible Church. I believe they want to address the matter of our property line." He looked back at the pastor, who gave Neil a go-ahead signal.

Neil stood and cleared his throat. "The church has been at its present location since its construction in 1942, and people have been parking in the present parking space. No one had any idea that the school's property line extended across and beyond the access road. The present members didn't build the church, and there's never been a reason to have the property surveyed."

"Are you saying it's the school's fault?" board member George Kirkman asked in an accusatory tone. Full of self-importance, George always jumped on any negative point he could find. Thankfully, Don Sawyer was president of the board rather than George.

Neil suppressed his irritation and kept his voice steady. "I'm saying nothing of the sort. I'm simply pointing out that this is an innocent mistake."

George's face had turned smug. "I guess we've got you over a barrel, huh?"

"The church and school are both integral parts of this community," the moderator broke in quickly." Then he spoke directly to Neil. "We understand your position. You may continue."

In concise terms and tone Neil went over the research he had done, presented his figures, and gave the moderator a plat of the piece of property the church needed. A number of questions followed, which he fielded to the best of his knowledge.

"We're prepared to purchase the property," he

concluded, and then stated an offer.

"Thank you, Mr. Bronson," the moderator said.

The superintendent, a burly man in his fifties, cleared his throat and signaled that he wanted to speak. "I appreciate the work you've done and the generous offer you've made, but I've been informed that the school cannot sell any property to individuals privately. It has to be done through a public auction."

Neil's gut wrenched. He hadn't anticipated that. He darted a quick glance at the pastor and received a nod that he took as a signal to use his judgment.

"Will it be auctioned in parcels or in one overall package?" he asked the superintendent. The church could not possibly buy an entire vacant school to get that little strip.

The man appeared thoughtful. "I think we can break it into parcels, but we'll have to have the surveyor plat it out."

"May we see the new survey when it's ready?"

The superintendent nodded. "We want to work with you people. We'll contact you so you can look at it prior to the auction."

"Thank you." Neil took his seat.

When Haley's hand pressed his in a quick gesture of approval, he wanted to hug her. Having her beside him made him feel like David, able to slay any giant. He swallowed past the lump in his throat. He would love to know what went on inside that pretty head of hers.

~

Haley's head spun with conflicting emotions—pride in the way Neil handled himself, and aggravation at

George's attitude. In a small town like this everyone knew everybody else's pasts and how to anticipate their actions. Neil may have been carefree growing up, but he had standards and treated others fairly and with respect. George, on the other hand, had a short temper and a need for attention. The only reason he had gotten elected to the board was that he had so much extended family and knew how to put on a good front prior to and during elections.

It seemed prophetic how Neil fit so smoothly into leadership at the church. For him it was a natural. Although they had talked about their relationship becoming serious, the possibility of him being in the ministry had Haley in a state of near panic.

It was a relief when the moderator announced that the board would now go into closed session, and they stood to leave.

Darlene Fowler caught up with them before they made it to the door, notepad and pen in hand. "What will the church do if the school won't sell you that strip of land?" Her facial expression made Haley think of a bumblebee on the attack.

"We'll ask the Lord to show us what to do," the pastor answered. A man truly called by God, his whole being radiated a confidence that boosted Haley's own assurance.

"It'll be handled professionally," Neil added as they headed for the door.

Chapter 14

$\mathcal{T}$he week passed quickly. Haley observed how well Neil kept the teenagers involved, and heard reports about the lively discussions and good times they were having building heaven. The youth adored and looked up to him. Church members respected him. Haley admired the way he lived his convictions and related to all age groups

He made no further mention of their relationship, and Haley sensed a reserve in him. She had no doubt he was spending a lot of time in prayer about his future. She just wasn't sure how— or if—she fit into it. He could be having second thoughts about her. He had to realize that her different background made her poor material for a pastor's wife.

By Friday night she was exhausted enough to welcome the end of Teen College—but excited enough about its success to hate having it end. Neil caught up with her in the parking lot as she reached her Tracker.

"Thank you for all your help. You made a huge contribution. The kids love you."

But do you? She watched in silence as he turned and walked to his Cherokee.

At home she had to convince Dillon to take it easy and not try to do too much too soon. He finally agreed to wait until the next week to resume his job search.

Saturday afternoon Haley decided they needed some family time. She pulled into the carport, parked, and dialed her sister, who was spending the weekend in town with her girlfriend.

"Come over and eat with Dillon and me," she said when Leann answered. "Dillon's cooking, and I've been to the grocery store and bought ice cream."

"I'll be right there."

Haley glanced behind her at the vehicle passing the house. For a moment she thought it was Neil's Cherokee. Drat. Why did she have to see him everywhere? Think of him every moment? Or think she did? She admitted she was head over heels in love with him, but her focus needed to stay on her work and her family. She sat there a little longer, trying to get a grip on her wayward emotions before heading inside.

"Leann's coming to supper," she announced as she entered the living room with her grocery bag. "Something sure smells good. What are we having?"

Dillon's smiling face appeared in the kitchen doorway. "I'm working on a meatloaf and mashed potatoes."

"Wow. You've turned into a world class chef." She kicked off her shoes, entered the kitchen, and put the ice cream in the freezer.

"Not for much longer."

She set down the bottle of ketchup she had started to put in the refrigerator and backed up to stare into his face. "What do you mean?"

His smile turned smug. "I won't have time. I won't be going hunting for a job any more either. I picked up your mail while you were out shopping. I'm going to work."

She turned to grab him in a bear hug.

"Hey, what's going on?" Leann's voice came from the doorway.

Dillon beamed. "I've got a job at the school, keeping their buses running."

Leann made it a group hug. Haley found it heartening. Her siblings were going to be able to take care of themselves. Mom would never take care of herself again.

~

Tuesday afternoon Neil couldn't believe his eyes. An auction sale bill stared at him from the window of a downtown shop. Not only had the school board not contacted him or shown him a copy of their new survey before moving ahead with their plans, but the advertisement was not correct. The property described on the sale bill was different from the drawing he had given the board and they had approved.

Frustration boiled up in him. He wanted to yell at someone. He tamped down on that urge and headed back to the funeral home, praying as he walked. When he arrived at the office, he called the superintendent.

When the administrator assured him that the sale bill was correct, Neil clamped down on his anger and informed the man that he would be at the office in five minutes to examine the plat.

An hour later, Neil returned to town more frustrated than ever. He checked his watch. Haley should be finishing her route about now. He drove to the post office and parked behind it to wait for her to arrive.

She had become such an important part of his life that he needed to share everything with her, even the bad, and find strength in facing things together.

When the mail truck pulled in, he tapped his horn to alert her to his presence. When she looked his way, he beckoned for her to join him. She signaled that she was going inside but would be right back.

He tapped the steering wheel as he waited for her return. Then he gripped it tightly and closed his eyes to pray. He was still praying when she slid into the seat beside him.

He opened his eyes. "Have you seen the sale bills?"

She nodded. "Yes, they're all over town. I thought about calling you, but I was on the move—and not sure what to say." Her voice held a note of panic. "Have you done anything or talked to anyone yet?"

He related his phone call and personal visit to the superintendent's office. "Someone decided that the church doesn't need all the property we want and changed the plat to include part of it in one of the other parcels to make it more valuable." He took his copy from the dashboard and handed it to her.

She looked it over. "But the part they moved has no value to anyone but the church," she said, her face crinkled in dismay.

"I explained that to the superintendent. To appease me, he followed me to the church and actually looked at the site for the first time. I showed him the boundaries and measured it again in his presence. He made notes and said he'll look into it some more."

Haley put the paper down and took off her cap to comb her fingers through her hair. Then she touched his hand. "We need to pray that he fixes it."

He nodded and bowed his head. Her grip tightened, telling him of the depth of her concern, as he prayed for guidance and placed the matter in God's hands.

"Amen," she repeated in a whisper when he finished.

He felt so much clearer headed, and more hopeful. "I'm going to call every single board member and discuss this with them."

She thought a moment. "I don't know if it'll help, but I'll do the same." She put her cap back on and opened the door. "I should go."

He nodded. "I'll pick you up at nine in the morning. We'll go to the auction together and grab lunch afterward."

She nodded, waved, and walked away.

~

"There's been quite a stir since the pastor announced his retirement plans Wednesday night," Haley said as she hopped into Neil's Cherokee Saturday morning. She looked so natural, comfortable yet lovely in simple jeans and a red blouse.

Neil swallowed a pillow-sized lump in his throat, every nerve in his body buzzing to life. It felt so right having her with him. Her low range voice soothed his nervousness over the auction.

He backed out of her drive and headed for the school. "They're pretty much in shock."

"By the end of the year they should be used to the idea. I think it was wise of him to do it this way and let them think and plan ahead. They'll soon see his joy in knowing his work is finished and prepare to move forward."

She was right, but he couldn't think about that today. He turned onto Main Street. "Even he is still in shock over this land matter."

Haley made a sympathetic shake of her head. "I can't believe that none of the school board members knew about the plat change."

His grip on the wheel tightened. "They promised that it would be corrected so the church can bid on what it needs. I hope they keep their word."

"The plats won't be the same as what's on the sale

bill, but the land will still be sold in three parcels. Is that right?"

"That's what they promised. The main parcel will contain the school building. The section that was the playground is to be sold separately. Then there's the strip alongside the church that we want to buy."

He pulled in at the school and parked, then looked around at the sparse crowd. "I expected more interest than this."

"Maybe this is good," she said, also scanning the lot. They got out and joined the gathering around the auctioneer's truck.

"We'll start with the furnishings," the auctioneer announced from the back of his truck, a small bullhorn in his hand. He indicated a bookcase next to the wall of the building. "All right, folks, who'll give me a hundred dollars for that useful item?"

Neil's stomach grew tighter as the sale continued. The pastor's arrival and presence helped.

The sale of the major tracts, when it came, started with the smallest parcel, the one the church wanted. When the auctioneer asked for an opening bid, Neil held his number card where it could be seen clearly. "Five hundred," he bid, not sure where to start.

"One thousand," a man he didn't recognize bid.

"Fifteen hundred."

Silence.

"Sold," the auctioneer said with a bang of his gavel when no more bids were forthcoming. "Now let's sell the second piece."

Neil raised a hand for attention. "You sold it to us

for fifteen hundred, but the church will pay two thousand dollars for the property," he announced when the auctioneer paused. "That's the amount the church offered before learning the property had to be sold at auction."

There was a smattering of applause.

"Thank you on behalf of the school," the auctioneer said, a beam spreading across his face.

Neil looked at the pastor, suddenly wondering if he had overstepped his role.

Bill smiled and nodded approval. "Hopefully we just bought some goodwill," he said in a whisper. "Good relations between the church and school are important."

Having no further interest in the sale, their little threesome exchanged silent signals that they were ready to leave.

Darlene Fowler caught up to them before they could get away. "How do you feel now?" she asked Neil, notepad in hand.

"Relieved," he responded with a smile. "It's good to have it resolved."

"Can you give me a quote for the paper?"

"I think you should get that from the pastor. He's getting ready to give them a check."

Darlene studied him a moment and then transferred her attention to the other man.

"The church purchased the needed parking strip for a fair price. The Lord has a way of working things out for the best," the pastor was saying as Neil and Haley walked away.

Neil noted Haley's somber demeanor once they were in the Cherokee. "Don't let Darlene's manner bother you."

She nibbled at her lower lip for a moment before raising her eyes to meet his gaze. "I may have made the situation worse rather than resolving it."

He frowned. "Care to tell me how?"

"I stopped by her office several days ago to talk to her."

"And?" he prodded when she didn't continue.

"I set her straight about the fact that I never had an intimate relationship with Rick and that I didn't know he was serious about her."

He rubbed a hand over his chin, debating whether to tell. Yes, she needed to hear it. "There's one thing you don't know. Rick meant to dump her."

Haley gasped. "Knowing she might be pregnant?"

"I don't know if he knew or not. When I confronted him about coming on to you while seriously involved with Darlene, he admitted that he really liked you and wanted to date you openly. He said he was going to break off with Darlene."

"You're serious?"

He stared out the windshield. "I've always suspected that he told her, and an argument is why he jumped on his motorcycle and sped into that semi."

She stared, dumbfounded. "You're just theorizing."

"About the argument part, but not about what he told me."

She shook her head. "This is too much to grasp."

He started the motor and headed back to her house, dreading what he had to do next.

~

Anxiety knotted beneath Haley's breastbone as Neil parked in her driveway and turned to face her. He had grown quiet and withdrawn as he drove her there. She watched him swallow, as if having difficulty speaking.

"My leave time has ended, and I have to go back to St. Louis." A muscle worked in his jaw. "I have to make some serious decisions and deal with my job."

Was this good-bye?

"I understand," she said, hardly able to speak. She wanted to beg him to not go, but she knew how selfish that would be. She searched for the right words. "We both need some time to think and make decisions about our future."

"I'll miss you."

She stepped out of the vehicle, already lonely as she watched him drive away.

The next morning Haley couldn't bring herself to attend the church where she might encounter Neil and have to endure more good-byes. Dillon had already told her he planned to go to church with his friend Justin, so she went to the nursing home and sat in on their early chapel service, which was conducted by local ministers or members of their staff before reporting to their own churches. Afterward, she wheeled her mother to the dining room. As she snapped a large bib around her mother's neck, she noticed Neil's dad pushing his wife's wheelchair to a table across the room. yShe looked back at her mom quickly, hoping Jim hadn't seen them.

But he had.

"Nice to see you, Haley."

His warm voice at her shoulder forced her to acknowledge him. "Hello, Mr. Bronson. How's Lillian?"

Jim shrugged. "About the same. She's healing, but it's slow. The disease has spread through her body. I wanted to ask about your brother. How is he doing?"

Now she produced a genuine smile. "He's staying with me and doing well. He has a job lined up at the school, and he's supposed to start in a few days."

"That's good to hear. Bring him by to see us sometime."

"You're welcome to visit us anytime," she said, unable to keep her eyes from darting around the dining room.

He read the look. "Neil left right after church."

Chapter 15

*N*eil's gut twisted as he sank back into the sofa cushions and stared at the muted television. His apartment was small but utilitarian, sparsely furnished. His interest level hovered around zero. So long as he had a bed to sleep in and a place to scrounge up an easy meal now and then, his needs were covered.

As memories washed over him, he wished he had been stronger back in high school, that he had not taken the route of least resistance and further damaged Haley's already low self-esteem. He should have stood up to his classmates and teammates and told them what a sharp gal she was, rather than ignoring their petty comments about her family.

She had forgiven him, but regret still ate at him.

Coupled with a strong work ethic, a sense of duty, and an IQ higher than his own, she would make any man an exceptional wife. The idea of her being married to anyone else made his heart wrench.

His remembered weakness made him question his worthiness to be a minister. Could God use such a person? He had known since his teens that the ministry tugged at him. He'd been shocked the first time the idea crossed his mind, frightened at the thought of such a responsible calling. He had tried to escape it by doing other work that made a difference to society, but no matter how much he poured himself into those jobs, that first tug just wouldn't go away.

Haley's face floated behind his eyes, her petite form and sparkling eyes. He swallowed hard, remembering the sensation of kissing her, of holding her close.

Needing solace, he reached over and picked up Beth's well-worn Bible from the coffee table. It was one of the few items of hers that he had brought to the apartment, leaving most of their belongings in storage back in Skyview. He flipped the pages, not sure what to read. A flash of yellow highlighting caught his eyes. He turned back and found the scripture Beth had marked, John 16:33. *I have told you these things, so that in me you may have peace. In this world you will have trouble. But take heart. I have overcome the world.*

She had written a note in the margin. *Help is always there.*

He had prayed until he no longer knew how to

phrase his prayers. When he prayed about the police chief job, he had no doubt he could handle it, but turmoil ate at him. When he prayed about the ministry, he wasn't so confident about how he would handle it, but he felt calm and peaceful. When he prayed about Haley, he felt calm in his love for her, but he still feared for her life. He loved her, and he thought she loved him. If they married, he couldn't deny her the joy of a family, but he couldn't bear the thought of her getting pregnant. He didn't think he could survive the loss of another wife.

The ringing phone broke into his reverie. He snatched it from the coffee table where he had tossed it and checked the caller ID. "Yeah, Eric."

"You'll want to know that Mom fell and broke her ankle, but you don't …"

"What? How could that happen?" he interrupted.

"She talked Dad into taking her outside for some fresh air. Said she was shriveling up from being cooped up inside for so long. He parked her wheelchair in the little gazebo, and when he turned his back for a minute she decided to get up and sit on the gazebo seat. She fell."

Neil raked a hand over his face. "You did right to call me. Dad can't handle her alone, and you can't do everything."

When they disconnected, he began to pack. He was needed in Skyview, and he had a call from God that he could no longer deny.

~

The two weeks since Neil's departure had passed

slowly for Haley. She worked every weekday and spent evenings cementing her fresh bond with her brother. She also made it a point to not miss any opportunity to spend time with her sister, who had grown more confident and seemed to be developing a direction for her life. But no matter how busy she stayed, Haley missed Neil. She missed his camaraderie, his crooked smile.

She tried to be realistic. She had known from the beginning that it was unwise to get involved seriously with him. They were too different, could never have made a lasting relationship work. He was beyond her reach. She was bound by duty and family dependencies—Leann's college expenses and all the things involved in acting as her mother's power of attorney. Dillon needed encouragement. She lacked the confidence necessary to be a pastor's wife. She wanted to trust God and wait on His timing, but she still yearned to see Neil.

"Go get some rest while I cook supper," Dillon ordered as she put away the lawn mower late Saturday afternoon. "You've already worked a full afternoon in this August heat, and you're beat."

"Thanks." She forced a laugh.

He tucked the weed eater inside the storage room off the carport and went inside the house. Haley wiped her sweaty face on her arm and started to follow him, but the short beep of a car horn stopped her. She turned and saw a gold colored Mazda pull up alongside the curb. Darlene Fowler sat behind the wheel. She parked and beckoned.

Cautious, but curious, Haley approached the car. Darlene leaned over and opened the passenger door. "Get in."

Haley hesitated, but then eased into the car, her stomach tight. Darlene couldn't be seeking her out for anything pleasant. Might as well get it over with. She directed a wary look across the seat.

"What's up?" She tried to inject a pleasant note into her voice.

"Nothing," Darlene said awkwardly, rubbing a finger along the steering wheel. "I just wanted to talk to you."

"What about?"

Darlene faced her and took a deep breath. "I think it's time to clear the air between us."

Haley studied the woman. She didn't look angry, or seem her usual haughty self. "I've already told you that I wasn't intimate with your boyfriend."

"I know," she said, sounding surprisingly subdued. "Maybe I always did. But I resented having him make a fool of me."

Haley started to speak, but paused when Darlene held up a palm.

"There's more." The movements of her mouth said she had to force herself to speak. "I thought I was special to Rick. I didn't find out about you until after his death. When I did, I hated both of you. It was a long time before I finally realized that he had fooled you, too. But I couldn't like you."

Haley didn't know what to say, so she kept quiet.

Darlene produced a wobbly smile. "I still don't

know if I like you, but I respect you. I've seen how hard you work, and how you relate to the kids around here." Her voice broke at mention of the kids, her mouth trembling.

Haley reached over and touched her hand. "It's all right."

Darlene gathered her composure and straightened in the seat. "It's not all right, but it's going to be. Things are going to change. That's why I came to see you."

Haley sat still, having no idea what to expect.

"I've been focused on my own problems so much that I've left Ricky free to roam the streets. I honestly didn't know he and Mickey were bullying younger boys." She shook her head and stopped to compose herself again.

Haley hated to see Darlene hurting, but she rejoiced that Ricky and Mickey would no longer be allowed to torment others.

"Mickey is grounded," Darlene continued after a moment. "His mother, who also happens to be single, is going to tighten the reins on him—like I am with Ricky. They'll both be too busy the rest of the summer to get into trouble. Anyhow, that goat they took ended up in the Bronson shed because Ricky put it there. With Mickey grounded, he was stuck with it and wanted rid of it. So he put it where he knew it would be found. I'm sorry for the trouble they've caused … and for the way I've treated you," she finished after a pause.

"I'm sorry, too," Haley said. "For both of us. And I appreciate your honesty," she added, slightly uncomfortable.

Seeming to recover, Darlene turned an appraising eye on Haley. "In order to do my job, I observe people."

Haley just nodded, having no idea where this was leading.

"You're so busy taking care of others that you don't take care of what you want and need. It's obvious Neil Bronson is besotted with you," she continued in a rush. "For once in your life, you should go after what you want. You do want him, don't you?"

Of all the things Darlene could have said, that was the last one Haley would ever have expected. She couldn't form a response.

"That's okay," Darlene said. "You don't have to say it. You've always kept things close to your chest. But I've seen the two of you together. It seems to me you need each other. I just saw him come out of the funeral home a while ago."

Haley struggled to keep her face impassive, startled that he was in town and she hadn't known. "I know you're observant, but you're ..."

"Right about this," Darlene cut her off, glancing at her watch. "Well, I've said what I came to say, and I need to run."

Haley eased the car door open and stepped out. "Thank you for coming." *I think.*

As she closed the door, Darlene drove away, leaving Haley standing there in bemusement. They would never be bosom buddies, but they could share the same space now. One thing struck Haley as significant. If she could bridge the gap with Darlene, she could, with God's help, handle anything, even being a pastor's wife.

As for Darlene's order to go after Neil, she didn't know what to think.

For once in your life, go after what you want.

Over and over, the words pursued her, all during supper and throughout the evening. Dillon kept a curious eye on her, but he didn't ask questions, evidently deciding she needed time to process whatever was bothering her.

What if what she wanted went against God's will?

Should she call Neil? Go see him? Go for broke and bare her heart to him? No. She couldn't chase after a man. She would be mortified if she did that and he told her to get lost.

Had he come back to stay? How long had he been here? Did he plan to contact her?

No matter what her stubborn heart wanted, she had to accept reality. The only reason he truly had to be here was to check on his parents. He could very well have decided to keep his job in St. Louis. If he were to declare that he loved her madly and wanted her to live with him in St. Louis, could she leave her mother?

Haley crawled into bed, the questions still hammering at her.

~

Sunday morning Dillon and Leann went to church with Haley. It was wonderful. They sat together in a pew near the back. The service was just starting when Jim Bronson walked up the aisle past them to his usual seat nearer the front. Neil followed and slipped in beside his dad.

During the song service Haley's eyes continually strayed to those broad shoulders up ahead, unable to prevent the sense of longing that suffused her.

Stop being foolish. Enjoy this time with your family.

The pastor stepped behind the pulpit and began his sermon.

"Humans have three crucial needs. We each need something meaningful to do."

I have a job I like.

"We need someone to love and care about, and to love us in return."

I have my family. Her eyes locked on Neil in spite of her best effort to resist.

"And we need a believable hope about the present and future."

Haley glanced at her siblings. Both seemed glued to the pastor's words. Good.

After the service Haley wasted no time exiting the pew, leaving Dillon and Leann behind in her rush. Calling herself a coward, she was halfway to the exit when a hand clamped onto her forearm. "Haley."

Neil's voice made her heart leap. She halted and gulped a fortifying breath before turning to face him. He was so handsome. So wonderful. So beyond her reach. Or was he? She tried to read his expression and couldn't.

"I need your help with something," he said, his deep voice music to her ears. "Dad and I promised to eat with Mom at the nursing home, and I see you're with your brother and sister. If I pick you up about two, will you run an errand with me? Unless you have other plans."

"No. After we eat, the afternoon is free."

His expression relaxed, and a smile emerged. "I'll see you at two." He went to rejoin his dad.

Suddenly too nervous, or excited, to cook, Haley faced her siblings in the aisle. "Do you mind if we just get carryout somewhere and take it to the house?"

"I thought maybe you were going with your boyfriend." Leann rolled her eyes and made a quick head movement toward the departing Bronson men.

"No, they're eating with Mrs. Bronson at the nursing home." Haley wasn't ready to explain her plans.

They stopped at the Chinese restaurant and filled containers from the buffet. Then they took them to Haley's house and ate. After they finished, Dillon went outside to tinker with his truck, and Leann left for Springfield.

Haley had just changed into khaki slacks and a pink blouse when Neil pulled into the drive. Dillon darted a questioning look across the yard as she climbed into the Cherokee. Then he smirked and stuck his head back under the hood of his truck.

When she had her seat belt buckled, Haley faced Neil. "Where are we going?"

He gave her his quirky little grin and reached into his coat pocket. He took out a key and handed it to her. "You're the girl with an address book in her head. I want you to find the house this key fits."

Haley stared down at the key. It had a tag attached to it. She turned it over and recognized the address. She looked up and saw a twitch of amusement at Neil's mouth.

"You ninny," she said when she realized he was teasing her. "You know exactly what house this key fits. That's the address of the Runyon place." She paused. "They moved last month when Don's job transferred him to Iowa. The house is vacant and listed for sale."

He started the engine and backed out of the drive. "You're right, Miss Human Address Book."

She handed the key back to him, and he tucked it in his pocket. "It's a nice home. What's your interest in it?" A thread of hope crept through her.

"I noticed something interesting about it." He turned left onto Main Street.

Haley didn't ask any more questions, not sure what to make of his behavior.

Neil drove into a residential neighborhood that consisted of middle class homes. He pulled to the curb before the Runyon house and cut the engine. Then he turned to face her.

Haley's throat locked and went dry. She saw his left eye twitch. Why, he was nervous, too. There was a message coming from him that she couldn't quite interpret.

"Are you moving back here?" she asked bluntly, hardly able to squeeze out the words.

He nodded. "I've submitted my resume´ to the

church's search committee. Whether or not they call me is up to God. The only thing I'm certain about is that it's time to come home."

Haley's heart rate accelerated. "You're well-known and respected here. You also have some preaching experience. I have no doubt they'll ask you to be their pastor."

"I've given my notice in St. Louis. I have to go back and work one more week to train my replacement. Then I'll be back permanently. I'll help Dad with the business, at least until the end of the year. Hopefully it will be sold by then. If it's not, and the church doesn't call me, I'll accept that as God's will and continue to run the business, or run for Chief of Police."

Haley tried to absorb his words, afraid to ask why he was sharing such personal details with her.

He indicated the house. "What do you think of this place?"

"It's a lovely home."

"I've viewed it with a realtor. Do you think it's lovely enough to live in it?"

"Of course."

"With me? As my wife?"

"You're sure you want to marry me?" She breathed deeply, unable to move a muscle. Drowning in the nearness of him, the scent of him, she watched his Adam's apple bob.

He reached for her hand and cleared his throat. "Do you love me?"

Her response was automatic, prompted by the long held reservoir of love that she couldn't control or deny. "Of course I love you."

He exhaled in a rush, as if exploding with relief. "Say that again."

"I love you, I love you," she repeated. The words were a choked cry.

Satisfaction lit his face and eyes. "I thought you might, hoped you did. But I was afraid you wouldn't admit it." He shifted in the seat and scooted toward her.

Haley offered no resistance whatsoever when he pulled her to him. She spoke into his chest. "I've loved you for years. I'll always love you. That's the real reason I couldn't stay here after I finished high school. You and Beth were such a perfect match, and the feelings I had for you were too much for me to handle if I stayed here."

He pulled back and tilted her chin up so he could look into her eyes. "I never suspected."

She met his gaze. "No matter where I went, I never found anyone else who interested me. I prayed that God would release me from loving you after you chose another. I blocked it out and finally felt cured. But then I met you again."

Her voice trailed off, and she traced a finger across the curve of his beloved cheekbone.

Neil dipped his head and gave her a kiss to which she responded with one of her own. When it ended, the world seemed brighter, sharper. She pressed her face into his chest and held onto him.

He turned her face up again. "I guess God had a plan, and a timeline. It's hard to comprehend having two such wonderful women love me."

Haley wove her fingers through his hair, reveling in the freedom to do so.

He searched her face. "I'll live with you in your house if you don't want to give it up, or if you don't like this one. Or we can find another altogether. It doesn't matter to me, so long as you marry me and live with me."

She shook her head. "I love this house. And mine's too small for us, for a family."

A shadow crossed his face. "I'm scared to death of you getting pregnant and of possibly losing you. But I love you enough to risk it if that's what you want."

"Let's leave that up to God." She gave him a quick kiss.

He heaved a sigh. "I'll always remember Beth and what we had. And what I lost. But you're my present, and I want to spend the rest of my life with you."

Her heart soared. "Starting when?"

His mouth curved. "As soon as possible."

She pursed her lips. "I think Dillon might like to stay in my house. He's going to work soon, and he seems to like the place. He might even decide to buy it. So the house is not a problem."

"How about a Thanksgiving wedding, since I'm so thankful?"

The words stole her breath. "I like the sentiment."

He nodded and pulled her face right up to his. "It's a perfect time for a new beginning."

Her face split into a broad smile, even as she blinked back tears. She was much surer of her self-worth, comfortable with the person God had made her. But soon she would be a new somebody—Mrs. Neil Bronson. Her heart swelled until she thought it would burst. Tears of joy spilled from her eyes.

"You got yourself a date. A wedding date."

His lips found hers again.

Epilogue

*T*winkling lights of red, green, and gold made a festive aisle of Main Street. Christmas trees stood in many of the store display windows, and over half of them had holiday scenes painted on the glass panes. The residential sections of town were just as festive, including the Bronson home.

Haley's heart swelled when she pulled into the drive and saw her husband atop a stepladder, adding yet another string of lights to the eave of the porch. He turned, a lazy smile spreading across his face. Seeing him do that more and more often over the past two years had brought joy to her heart.

She grabbed the plastic bag from the passenger seat and hopped out of the Tracker. A tiny boy, bundled up in coat, hat, and mittens, sat on the porch in front of the door. When he saw her, he put his hands to the floor and worked his way to his unsteady feet. "Mama."

He shot forward, and then came to an abrupt halt, landing back on his bottom. His face puckered, and he howled.

Neil stepped off the ladder and reached him at the same time Haley did. He picked up the baby and unsnapped the leash fastened to the back of his pants. The other end was attached to the door handle.

"What's the matter, sweetheart?" Haley put her arms around the child, cuddling him sandwich-like between her and Neil.

"He's in custody." Neil straightened the cap on his head. "Isn't that right, scamp?"

Haley drew back, loving the sight of her handsome husband holding his eleven-month-old offspring. "What's the charge?"

"He swiped my shoe."

She put a hand over her mouth to hide a smirk. "But you found it …"

"In the kitchen trash can," they chorused in unison.

Haley held out her arms, and Neil passed the child to her.

"Poor Josh," she crooned, hugging her son. "My tiny criminal. Did you make your daddy's day off an exciting one?"

Neil's chuckle made her look up. When she did, he planted a quick kiss on her mouth. No matter how many times he did that, it always made her insides turn to a puddle of warm sensation.

"We went shopping," he said when he lifted his head. "Then we played games."

He peered down at the plastic bag still gripped in Haley's right hand. "Mmm. What kind of goodies did you bring home today?"

Josh's face did an instant transformation at the word goodies, and his fist came out. "Goo-ee," he squealed. Little fingers opened and closed repeatedly.

"You two are so spoiled," Haley accused, but she was smiling. A few people left treats in their mailboxes for her all year round, but during the holidays the expressions of appreciation and holiday cheer appeared in abundance.

She handed the bag to Neil. "We have cookies, nuts, and a cheese ball."

He extracted a cookie and gave his son a piece of it. "Say thank you."

Josh immediately planted a sloppy smooch on Haley's cheek. Then he stuffed his mouth full of cookie.

Neil broke off a chunk and put it between Haley's lips. "We love you, sweet mail lady."

The words were said easily, but with sincerity. He plucked a stray crumb from her chin and put it in his own mouth. "Hmm."

Haley tipped her head. "Who would ever have thought the love of my life would be my pastor?"

Pastor Bill had retired as planned, and the church had asked Neil to succeed him. Not only had Neil found peace in following God's plan, but he was truly happy and beloved by his congregation.

The tough times for him had been the months of her pregnancy. He had tried to hide his anxieties, but Haley had known. Josh's birth had been a double blessing for him, relief at her continued health, and the thrill of fatherhood.

Haley swallowed the bite of cookie and looked up at him, loving everything she saw. She drew a deep breath. "Are you ready for another one?"

Neil went still, his eyes sweeping over her from head to toe. "Are you saying what I think you are?"

She nodded.

A smile split his face. "I hope this one's a girl, one who looks just like you."

"What if she helps Josh swipe your shoes and throw them in the trash?"

He grinned. "Together you and I can handle anything."

The End

What is Kelsey to do
when she meets Nick Lafferty—
and discovers his connection
to the brother she is seeking?

Find out in
KELSEY'S KEEPER,
Last of this four book series,
Coming soon.

Books by Helen Gray

Mozark Marriages Series
>Ozark Sweetheart
>Ozark Reunion
>Ozark Wedding

Dodge City Duos Series
>Bandit Bride
>Prairie Bride

Heartland Heartmates Series
>Show Me Love
>Heartland Illusions
>Mozark Vision
>Missouri Catch

Boothill Beloveds Series
>Bootheel Bride
>Bootheel Bachelor
>Bootheel Betrothal

River Town Romance
>2 stories in 1 (Hawthorn Hope and Tree of Hope)

Lake Ozark Ladies Series
>>Paige's Proposal
>>Brooke's Bargain
>>Haley's Hero
>>Kelsey's Keeper